WORDWINGS

Sydelle Pearl

**GUERNICA
EDITIONS**
TORONTO • BUFFALO • LANCASTER (U.K.)
2017

This is a work of fiction based upon historical events.
Rivke and her diary are products of the author's imagination.

Michael Mirolla, editor
David Moratto, cover and interior design
Cover Image: Milk Can used to store
the Underground Archive of the Warsaw Ghetto
Reproduced with permission from the Archive Collection
of The Emanuel Ringelblum Jewish Historical Institute in Warsaw
Guernica Editions Inc.
1569 Heritage Way, Oakville, (ON), Canada L6M 2Z7
2250 Military Road, Tonawanda, N.Y. 14150-6000 U.S.A.
www.guernicaeditions.com

Distributors:
University of Toronto Press Distribution,
5201 Dufferin Street, Toronto (ON), Canada M3H 5T8
Gazelle Book Services, White Cross Mills
High Town, Lancaster LA1 4XS U.K.

First edition.
Printed in Canada.

Legal Deposit—Third Quarter
Library of Congress Catalog Card Number: 2017936270
Library and Archives Canada Cataloguing in Publication
Pearl, Sydelle, author
Wordwings / Sydelle Pearl. -- 1st edition.

(Essential prose series ; 142)
Includes bibliographical references.
Issued in print and electronic formats.
ISBN 978-1-77183-196-3 (softcover).--ISBN 978-1-77183-199-4
(Kindle).--ISBN 978-1-77183-197-0 (EPUB)

I. Title. II. Series: Essential prose series ; 142

PS3616.E13W67 2017   813'.6   C2017-901739-X   C2017-901740-3

To the memory of Dr. Emanuel Ringelblum,
founder and director of the Underground Archive
of the Warsaw Ghetto; to those who contributed
their words and their artwork to this Archive;
to those who were entrusted with burying it under
the earth; and to those who painstakingly searched
for this Archive under the rubble of the
Warsaw Ghetto after the Second World War
in their determination to bring it to the light of day.

Note to Readers

In the rubble that was left of the Warsaw Ghetto after the Second World War, in a large aluminum milk can buried deep in the earth, part of the Underground Archive was discovered. Among many other intriguing documents, the diary of twelve-year-old Rivke Rosenfeld was found wrapped in a rag, alongside of a folded burlap sack containing tiny cloth puppets. Under the diary were hundreds of portraits of children made by the Ghetto artist Gela Seksztajn.

The diary has been translated from Polish into English and is herewith published in its entirety.

9 January 1941

FOR A LONG time, I lie in the darkness and feel my own heart beating like a thousand angry birds trapped within my chest. I wish to scream and sob and run away. But there are five other people sharing this sanctuary with me. Their bodies lie still except for the rise and fall of their breathing. It is so cold that they shiver in their sleep and pull at the rags and coats that serve as blankets.

From the table that once held the Torah, I reach for my white armband with the blue Star of David and slip it upon my coat sleeve, near my elbow. Then I pull out a book with a torn cover from inside of my pillow. There are thirteen stories by Hans Christian Andersen, and I have read this book so many times that I know the stories by heart. I kept asking Batya if I could take it out from the library again and again until she finally told me I could keep it.

But I am not thinking of reading stories now. I must find something to write with—my hand aches to grasp a pen or a pencil. I remember Zayde's measurements that he makes with a pencil so he knows how much cloth to cut for making pillows and armbands. In the dark, my fingers and my feet guide me past the bodies of my sisters, Tsipoyre and Sorele, to my grandfather's little cart leaning against the side of the room. Next to the cart, I hear Zayde snoring. Gittel Goldman and her twin sister Ruchel also share this small sanctuary with us. In the large sanctuary upstairs, there are thirty-five people. It is no wonder that the toilets stopped working months ago. The icy air dulls the horrible stench, and even though it is so cold, we keep a window open a bit to help ourselves breathe.

Attached to Zayde's cart, I find his little bundle of sewing tools wrapped in a piece of dirty cloth. Carefully, I carry it to my thin straw mattress. I wrap my scarf around my head and neck, and I push up the sleeves of my coat so that they won't be in the way. Inside the cloth, there are three spools of thread, a pair of scissors, two needles that I prick my thumb on, and a short, stubby pencil. This pencil is a precious thing to me, and I hug it with my fingers.

I take a deep breath and open my book. In the dark, I begin to write, and those angry fluttering birds pushing against my chest fly away.

I pray that I can write clearly and small enough in between the margins so that my words will stand out from the print. I write with the hand that bears the armband. The armband must be witness to my words. I wish to write in Yiddish, but I don't know it well enough, although I can speak it. I write in Polish — the same language as the stories.

Even though it is night, I close my eyes for a moment to see the picture in my mind of the Puppet Beggarman,

Mr. Tuchman, Mrs. Rotstejn, and especially Zayde. When I open my eyes again, tears are sliding down my face into the folds of my scarf. My tears are silent while my hand holding the pencil screams.

Here is my memory:

I am standing behind Zayde's cart with the pillows and the folded white armbands with the blue Star of David sewn upon them. It begins to snow, and I raise my face and arms towards the sky as though I have wings. For a moment, I close my eyes and imagine myself transformed into a great white swan flying over the wall and barbed wire of the Ghetto until I arrive in a beautiful green meadow very far away—somewhere in a Hans Christian Andersen fairytale.

But it is so cold that the wind pricks my fingers, and I put them underneath the armbands in the cart, where I find Tsipoyre's hands already burrowed like rabbits. We laugh and then settle there, grasping each other's hands for warmth. I glance at Sorele sitting on Zayde's lap, her brown curly hair twirling in the wind. She is wearing white gloves tinged with blue scraps that Zayde has made for her. She is holding her rag doll, Margarita, another gift from Zayde.

Most people pass by the market on Gesia Street in a hurry, buried in their coats, sweaters, or rags. People are lined up on both sides selling clothes, pots, pans, books, pieces of coal, scraps of wood. Some peddlers carry their wares in their hands or in baskets in front of them. There is a man in the distance holding a handful of balloons.

Beggar children follow him and reach out for the dangling strings. The colors dance in front of my eyes. Red, blue, green. I have never seen balloons in the Ghetto before. Where did he get them? The colors make me try to remember flowers, the river, trees.

There is an old woman wearing a kerchief who clutches apples to her chest, and I wonder if she is truly able to sell them and let them go. A beggar, with his beard wrapped around his neck like a scarf, limps slowly along as though he is in pain, and I notice that he has no shoes—his feet are wrapped in burlap. A burlap bag hangs over one shoulder. He holds one hand in front of him like a little cup, while the other one is wearing a kind of glove puppet that looks something like him, with its long gray beard and the little sack hanging over one shoulder. As the man passes, his little puppet bows to me, its tiny blue hat bobbing in greeting, and I am so enchanted that I watch the two of them with my mouth wide open. The puppet's coat is torn just like the man's, and the threads of both become entangled and dance in the wind.

I make up a story in my mind about him. I imagine that he is the Peddler of Wind. He travels with his puppet, their sacks of wind over their shoulders. Perhaps they carry many different kinds of wind. Warsaw Ghetto wind. American wind. Chinese wind. Fairytale wind. He can even climb over the Ghetto wall to smuggle in the Aryan wind from the Other Side. I imagine the two sacks filled to bursting with magic wind.

Then he begins to chant in the high voice of his puppet: "A bisele broyt. A bisele broyt. A bit of bread. A bit of bread ..." And my thoughts about his magic wind vanish. The Yiddish words seem to stick to my ears, and I wish to shake my head to rid myself of the sound of them.

Suddenly, my stomach tightens as though someone has punched it. Making his way in our direction, I see a tall, pimple-faced German soldier taking measured footsteps in the snow with his shiny, black boots. The soldier trips the Peddler of Wind on his one good leg, and he lands with a sigh onto the frozen ground. In that moment, he ceases his chanting and pushes himself slowly along on his hands and knees, until he turns out of sight at the corner of Smocza Street.

The soldier continues his measured strides and pauses when he gets to Mr. Tuchman's bookcart, right near Zayde's. He opens up book after book with his gloved hands and rips out pages and pages of Hebrew and Yiddish words. Some of the books that he destroys are children's books. The strong wind carries their bright pictures across the Ghetto.

The soldier makes harsh barking sounds, and his lips curl into a strange sort of smile, so I guess he must be laughing, even though it sounds like he is choking. Mr. Tuchman's face turns white. His eyes grow so wide with fear I wonder if they will leave their sockets entirely.

"Pick them up! Pick up all the Jewish pages!" shouts the soldier. "Mach schnell! Quickly!" His German reminds me of Yiddish but his words make me shiver.

Mr. Tuchman turns around wildly to catch the pages that he can. As he bends down to pick up a book from the snow, the soldier kicks him with his heavy boot.

Mr. Tuchman is thrust to the ground and his eyeglasses fall off his face. His wife hands him his glasses, wraps her arm around him, and they begin to walk away—both of them bent over with grief.

The soldier stands there with his hands on his shiny belt buckle and laughs. Another German soldier holding a dog on a leash marches over and salutes him with "Heil Hitler!" Together, they coldly eye all of us along Gesia Street. We are very quiet and very still. Each of us tries to look invisible. I find a spot on the ground near one of the books lying in the snow and I stare at it. My heart is beating so furiously I think that it can be heard from miles away. But then I wonder how my heart can beat at all if I feel as frozen as a statue.

I force myself to move. I squeeze Tsipoyre's hands, and she squeezes mine back from under the pile of armbands and pillows.

Carefully, I grasp as many armbands as I can and thrust them into the pockets of my coat. Tsipoyre follows my example. Zayde has Sorele stand up. Then he turns over the box they were sitting on and stuffs as many pillows inside of it that will fit. The few pillows that do not fit into the box, Zayde stuffs under his coat. He turns the box over again and sits down with Sorele on his lap, both of them trembling.

The two soldiers take their time, walking in a stiff march up and down the street—our marketplace. They point to Mrs. Rotstejn who is selling her potatoes, holding out her apron in front of her coat like a table. The dog sniffs at her. She steps backwards as if to get away and they grab her arms—one on one side and one on the other until she cries out with pain. They release her when her coat rips at the armpits. She places her apron over her face to hide her sobs. Meanwhile, her potatoes drop onto the snow. They are probably rotten anyway—most of them just peelings. But even a potato peel helps keep hunger away in the Ghetto.

The soldiers pick up the potatoes and peelings. Using their knives from their pockets, they cut this food into tiny pieces and throw them onto the snow in all directions. A few Jews scramble to gather what they can, while the soldiers laugh so hard they pat each other on the back.

"Dogs! Jewish dogs!" they scream. The real dog beside them barks and growls menacingly.

Then it is our turn. I cling to Tsipoyre's hand behind the cart. Sorele hugs Zayde tightly.

The two young German soldiers with shiny belt buckles and crisp heels march in our direction. They carry their guns against their shoulders. On the sleeves of their uniforms, I can see the twisted black cross of the swastika. Snowflakes fall onto their helmets and disappear.

They stop in front of our cart. I can see the breath of the panting dog hanging in the air like steam. One of the soldiers points at Zayde and orders him to come towards him. Zayde gently lifts Sorele from his lap. She steps between me and Tsipoyre, her arms encircling us both.

Zayde does not look at the soldiers directly, but he nods and takes off his hat with one hand. His chin trembles slightly. He places the four pillows from under his coat on top of the empty cart. He stands at the side of it. The soldiers hold up the pillows and examine them. Zayde has embroidered beautiful patterns on the front and back. On the front, there is the outline of the Vistula River with flowers growing and ducks swimming. The back of each pillow shows the sliver of the moon and a wavy outline of the shimmering water.

The soldiers turn the pillows around from front to back and back to front. The one with the pimples on his face takes a knife from his pocket and rips a pillow open. The soldiers look surprised. The pillows are so beautiful on the outside that they expect feathers inside of them instead of rags.

The soldiers take off their gloves and pinch Zayde's face until it is very red. Then they forcefully pull down on Zayde's beard. But it does not leave his face easily, and the soldiers become impatient. Using their knives, they cut it off, along with some skin. When Zayde's chin begins to bleed, I feel my own face burning from the wind, the cold, and my anger. I am sure his legs will collapse but then he holds his body very straight and does not flinch. Tsipoyre, Sorele, and I hardly breathe.

The soldiers put their knives in their pockets and step away from Zayde. A few straggly hairs hold onto his chin. Blood drips onto the white snow and remnants of his gray beard swirl around in the wind. Will a bird make a nest from my grandfather's beard?

My zayde's fingers reach up to touch his wounded face. The soldiers take turns spitting in his eyes and he blinks. He holds his back even straighter. Tsipoyre holds her head high and digs her nails into my palms to keep me from rushing towards them in my fury. Sorele buries her head under my coat.

The soldiers laugh and laugh. The dog barks and barks.

We Jews lower our eyes and are silent. People glance at my zayde and then look away. The soldiers start to march—one foot following the other in their shiny boots, the dog with its tongue hanging out of its mouth, panting. They are finished playing with us for now.

When they are out of sight, Tsipoyre, Sorele, and I reach for our grandfather. He sits upon the box filled with pillows, and Sorele wraps her arms around him like she never will let go. Tsipoyre hugs both of them. They make room for me when I take some armbands from my pocket and place them around Zayde's face. The white cloth turns red and sticks to his chin. I cover his head with kisses. When I take a breath, I am tasting the salt of tears, and my grandfather is the one kissing my cheek. His lips are cracked and rough. I love him so much.

There we are—Tsipoyre, Sorele, Zayde, and I clinging to each other. And I think of those oak trees that I have seen in Saski Park, not far from where we used to live. The Jews are forbidden to go there. But sometimes I stop to look through a crack in the Ghetto wall, and I can see those trees. Even when I close my eyes, I can see those trees in my mind. Our love is like that. It is deep like the earth where the roots of those trees reach down, strong like the thick branches that grow, and endless like the sky.

I tiptoe over my sleeping sisters until I am near Zayde's cart. I kiss his shorn face, still wrapped in the armbands. The pencil presses against my fingers and I know that I cannot put it back tonight. It is small enough for me to clench in my fist like a secret weapon.

Somehow, I must get my own pen or pencil. No one must see me write. If those German soldiers knew I wrote down everything about how they treat us, they would shoot me in a second. I will pretend I am a bird with invisible wings. No one will know that I can fly away in my imagination.

The Warsaw Ghetto has turned us all into birds. Like sparrows, we walk gingerly upon the frozen ground, eyes darting nervously from side to side as we cross one dirty street to another. Like pigeons, we peck at the ground searching for crumbs of bread. Like seagulls, we long to glide on the wind.

I am very tired. I have written for a long time. The light from the sun creeps into this room from underneath the heavy window shade.

I will slip the book of Hans Christian Andersen stories against my bare skin where someday my nipples will grow into breasts. I wonder what it would feel like to grow feathers.

Before I close this book, I imagine that I plant my words deep into the ground, like the roots of a secret tree. Then, in the soil that covers my words, I sow flower seeds—red roses, purple violets, and yellow sunflowers. And in the soft magic wind, my words and the words of

Hans Christian Andersen push up through a crack in the dirt and turn themselves into wings.

My stomach rumbles and wakes me up. I try to forget my hunger and reach for this pencil and book once again. It is so cold that my teeth chatter.

One of Tsipoyre's songs comes into my head. Since we have moved into this Ghetto, I have not heard her sing. Her songs used to carry us all from Shabes to Shabes. But now, barely a word passes between her lips. When she does speak at all, her voice sounds like a rough stone.

Do you recognize yourself, my shvester, my sister? I will help you find your soul again. Whenever I think of one of your songs, I will write it down.

Remember when I told you the story of the poor shepherd boy who didn't even know the Hebrew alphabet? He spoke to God in his own way, and you wrote a song about him.

> *I can see the sun setting*
> *Behind the hills.*
> *I can feel the wind blowing*
> *From far away.*
> *I can hear the cows mooing—singing their song.*
> *I can pick up my reed pipe and play along.*
> *Oh, dear God, I don't know how to pray.*
> *But I'll sing you this song anyway.*
> *Oh, dear God, I don't know how to pray.*
> *But I'll sing you this song anyway.*

Your song inspires me to make up my own prayer. Dear God, I say in my mind, Watch over us.

Watch over Sorele. She is still filled with some wide, peaceful place inside of her. It is as if she carries inside of her some of the grasses from the field near our old house in Praga. I have told her so much about it, she has made the pictures her own.

And Grandfather must continue to sew and sew as long as he is able, for he sews pillows as well as memories. His thread binds us all together. With scraps of thread he has left, he embroiders little pictures on his pillows, pictures that even surprised the Nazi soldiers who stole his beard.

"Look at that!" someone will say as he notices an embroidered pillow on the cart. And Zayde will tell about the flowers that grew in the field when he was a boy or the horse he rode when he was a traveling tailor. For an instant, it may be possible to forget about the narrow, crowded, dirty streets with the never-ending stench.

I think of Zayde sewing with his needle outside in "God's Field," the name he called the park that was near our home in Praga. When I was small and wanted to help him, he took my little hands in his big ones and showed me how to work the needle. Up and down, up and down we went together, as though we were the wind rippling over the cloth. Sometimes, I would prick my finger and it would bleed. "Let me kiss it," he'd say, and it would feel better.

One day, when it rained suddenly, we had to hurry and bring all of the cloth and thread into the house. I told my grandfather that I wanted to sew coats for the flowers so that they would be protected from the rain.

"Ah, but they need the rain," Zayde said. "They love to drink it up the way that you love to drink up milk from Janina."

Janina was our goat. How I loved to drink her milk! She looked like a rabbi, I thought, with her wise eyes and her beard. I imagine her living in the Warsaw Ghetto with us and wearing a Jewish star, too. I would have to teach her not to run on these crowded Ghetto streets.

But I have not been to Praga since I was eight years old and Tsipoyre was six. Now I am twelve and Tsipoyre is ten. Sorele wasn't even born yet when we moved to Warsaw so that Papa could get a better job as a teacher.

Zayde turns over in his sleep, and the floorboards creak. Does the raw skin on his chin ache under the armbands? He sleeps with his tallis wrapped about him, underneath his tattered blanket, like a prayer.

Sorele sleeps with her rag doll, Margarita. Margarita's dress is adorned with embroidered roses, and her hair is made from a scrap of brown burlap. Zayde has even made shoes for her out of pieces of cardboard. Sorele is only four years old—too young to wear an armband, but even so, she has asked Zayde to sew a tiny one on the sleeve of Margarita's dress.

The Nazis do not allow us to study, but I walk with Tsipoyre and Sorele to one of the children's kitchens down the street at Nowolipki 68. The teacher, Estera, tries hard to make it a pleasant place. Children come from

Grodzisko, Skierniewice, and Lodz as well as Warsaw.
The families of Warsaw have lost their homes, like us.
Many children look familiar to me. I have seen them
begging on the streets. All of us have lost our parents in
this terrible war. We are the lucky ones because we have
Zayde. Children come with real shoes and others come
with rags tied around their feet. Some of them walk
barefoot in the snow like Hans Christian Andersen's little match girl.

There is some hot oatmeal to eat. When everyone
is finished, Estera beckons us to sit in a circle on a blanket on the floor, and she sings songs in Yiddish about
trees, flowers, and sunshine as if to keep the cold away.
Little voices sing along. I watch Tsipoyre nod her head
in rhythm, but she doesn't sing the words—not yet. We
are older than most of the children, but we need to be
together with Sorele. There are other sisters and brothers who come together and cannot be parted.

One little ivy plant sits on the windowsill and grows
in spite of the frost. The children love that plant. They
talk about how someday it will grow very tall, so I tell
them the story of "Jack and the Beanstalk."

Estera lifts the cloth that hides a bookshelf. Children sit on scattered pillows in front of it. We all know
to place the books on the shelf and pull down the cloth
if a German soldier enters suddenly. It has not happened
yet, but whenever Estera stomps on the steps, that is our
cue to practice. The room becomes very still as we scramble to lie down on the worn rug or upon a pillow to pretend that we are napping.

I always lie down between my two sisters and turn my head so I can see the cloth we have decorated with suns, moons, and flowers—with hope.

Estera claps her hands and says that we have done such a good job of hiding and pretending. She is very proud. I think we are like peacocks hiding beautiful feathers.

Sometimes Batya comes from the library and reads stories and leaves books. The children turn the pages again and again, pointing and murmuring to themselves.

I read aloud to children who wish to hear more stories in Polish and Yiddish. I forget about the cold and the misery and read with my heart. One time, I pick my head up to see Batya looking at me curiously. I have just finished "Puss in Boots."

There is a folded map of the world on the bookshelf. I open it up and point to Poland first, especially the squiggly line that is the Vistula River. Then I point to France, where the story comes from. I point to Denmark, too—the home of Hans Christian Andersen and his stories.

The map is ripped on the folds because we look at it again and again. This would make the Nazis very angry. They forbid us to learn about the world but they cannot stop us. I fly all around the sky like a bird, in my imagination.

I excuse myself to the children and go find out what Batya wants to tell me.

"You read very well, Rivke. Such expression! Perhaps you can help me bring books to the children of the Ghetto a few times a week?"

"Yes," I tell her. "This is what I would love to do!" We arrange to meet at the children's library at Leszno Street 67 on Monday morning.

How strange that I don't feel hungry anymore! I think about Hans Christian Andersen's little match girl — how, before she dies from the cold, she strikes match after match and has the most beautiful visions. She sees a warm stove, a table full of food, a sparkling Christmas tree, and finally, her grandmother.

This book and pencil are like my own box of matches. My words can warm me, take me far away, and still my hunger and my anger.

Before I slip this book inside of my pillow, I make up a new prayer. Dear God, I say. Watch over me as I write.

17 January 1941

I SMOOTH OUT my armband with the Jewish star that is on the sleeve of my coat. My hand trembles with eagerness to catch my words.

I am writing with the pen that Batya has given me. I volunteer to help her bring books to children on the streets, in the orphanages, kitchens, and apartment houses. She does not let me bring books to children in the hospital since she is afraid I'll come down with typhus. But the lice that carry the deadly disease are everywhere. The posters on the Ghetto wall say: "Typhus! Beware!" Some of them show a Jew with a big nose and a long beard with a louse peering out of it. The caption below is: "Jews are crawling with the Typhus." The insulting posters are ripped off as soon as they appear, but is it any wonder that without proper food, clothing, soap, or water we get sick?

Batya and I each carry a briefcase filled with children's books that we give away when children return the books to us that they have already read. We must clean the books when we get them back with a certain strong-smelling liquid soap. When they are covered with lice, we mustn't touch them. Batya has them burned.

I am flooded with memories of the typhus epidemic

two months ago that took the lives of so many people including our parents and our bubbie, our grandmother. How their bodies were covered with the red sores and how they burned from the fever!

Miraculously, Sorele, Tsipoyre, Zayde, and I did not get sick. We had to pretend that nothing was wrong. If the Nazis had found out about Bubbie, Mama, and Papa, we would have been forced to remain in the sanctuary for at least two weeks. Someone would have had to bring us our rations of thin soup and bread. But the Nazis are always so afraid of germs, they might have taken us somewhere far away. So we decided it was best to keep the sickness a secret as long as possible. Zayde insisted that Tsipoyre, Sorele, and I move up to the large prayer hall.

At that time, Gittel and Ruchel weren't living with us in the synagogue. I think they were hiding on the Aryan side of Warsaw. They look so alike that whenever I have seen them together I find myself staring at their blonde hair and blue eyes. Gittel has a mole on the side of her face — it is the only way I can tell them apart.

By the time we returned to the small sanctuary, they had come back, too. I wondered what their lives had been like since we last saw them. I wanted to ask them questions, but I wasn't sure I wanted to know the answers. What is it like on the Other Side? Where do you stay? Are you smugglers? Do you pretend to be Polish?

I didn't know how to ask these questions, but I wanted to let them know of our sorrow. I knew they hid their own troubles. A few months ago, their parents were shot for not wearing armbands. Now they only had each other.

Their parents had been teachers in Papa's school. Gittel and Ruchel had been Papa's students.

When I told them how Mama, Papa, and Bubbie had died, they put their hands over their eyes and wept. Then Gittel shook her hair away from her face and wiped her hands on her coat. She reached into her pockets and brought out four apples. One of them had a little green leaf still clinging to it, and that was the one she gave to me. Ruchel reached into her knapsack and pulled out white rolls as big as her hands.

"The food cannot bring your family back," Gittel said, "but it will give you strength to live another day. And to live is to fight."

Zayde said a prayer and we munched silently on the apples, licking our lips to catch the juice. I took a deep breath, hoping to remember the sweet smell forever.

Gittel and Ruchel joined us, munching on their own apples that they miraculously lifted from their magic pockets. They smiled as they chewed, and I noticed that their eyes were kind.

I remembered Batya's kind eyes. She came to the large prayer hall with her briefcase filled with books. Her knock was gentle on the door, and when she came in, I wanted to hug her, kiss her, and thank her for the wonderful fairytales from faraway continents like Africa and Australia. But I was afraid to pass along any germs to her, so I could only smile, nod, and hold out my arms for the books. Tsipoyre reached for them eagerly and Sorele jumped up and down with joy. She couldn't wait to look at the pictures and hear Tsipoyre or me read to her. The few children who lived in the large prayer hall gathered around to look at the books, too. Those books helped us to feel strong.

Zayde argued with Tsipoyre, Sorele, and me on the staircase, telling us not to enter the small sanctuary. But we missed Mama, Papa, and Bubbie so much that he finally allowed us to come down for a short visit. I read those fairytales aloud and felt my whole family listening intently.

As we made our way up those steps to the large sanctuary, I could hear Zayde continuing with the stories where I left off. Upstairs, Tsipoyre, Sorele, and I kept ourselves away from the other families. We didn't want anyone to get sick. When the children asked about the storybooks, I told them I would tell them stories myself. I told Hans Christian Andersen's "The Nightingale" again and again during those few weeks. It seemed to be the only story I could recall. The sick emperor managed to get well in that story, and the soothing songs of the nightingale enchanted Death so much that, even though he sat on the emperor's bed, he drifted outside to see the lovely forest described in the nightingale's songs.

Towards the end, Mama, Papa, and Bubbie told us to leave their bodies out in the street where the funeral carts would find them and wheel them away. There was nothing we could do. No doctor could help us. They were so busy with the sick that many of them took ill themselves. There was no medicine and no room in the hospital. The one thing we were able to do was take rags, dip them into water, and place them on their burning limbs.

Their collective wish was to die together, holding hands. And so they did. The man attending to the funeral carts had to separate their fingers before lifting them onto the pile of other bodies.

"*Live! Live!* You must do your best to live! Help one another to survive!" they whispered hoarsely when we put the compresses on them. Their lips were dry and cracked. Their tongues hung out of their mouths as they gasped for breath.

I say to them in my mind, I *am* living. Zayde, Tsipoyre, Sorele, and I are all living. Thank God. Are your spirits watching over us? I am keeping you alive with my words.

Mama—the way your long red hair hung down your back. So soft and wavy and shiny. Papa loved to comb it out after you washed it before every Shabes. The children you worked with loved to play with it, too. You sang them lullabies of your own, and they wanted to rock on your lap long after it was time to go home.

Papa—your eyes were so bright and deep. Your voice was always filled with music. Even when you said ordinary things like: "Put on your shoes, my girls. Put on your coats."

Thank God you can't see us now. Our shoes are beginning to resemble shmates, rags. We stick bits of cloth and burlap in between our laces to help keep our feet warm.

Oh Papa—your students loved to eat lunch with you so that you could tell them more Peretz stories.

*I remember the story you used to tell about a poor
husband and wife who have nothing with which
to celebrate Passover. Rivke-Bayle is crying when
Chaim-Yona returns from the synagogue. He tells
her to dry her tears. God will provide. He reminds
her that on this holiday it is said at every table:
"Let all who are hungry, come and eat!" They are
about to leave their tiny hut to try to find a Jewish
home where they may share a meal. Rivke-Bayle
has just draped her torn shawl over her shoulders,
and Chaim-Yona has just opened the door, when
a voice they have never heard before wishes them a
good holiday. Elijah the Prophet, disguised as a
magician, enters their hut. Magically, he brings to
life candles and candlesticks, soft pillows to recline
upon, a white tablecloth covered with delicious
food to eat, along with matzah, wine, the seder
plate, and even a Hagaddah—the book that
contains the story of Passover. The husband and
wife are astonished and frightened. They rush
to the home of their rabbi and ask him if it is
permissible for them to partake of the food. The
rabbi tells them to go home and see if they can taste
the wine, sit on the pillows, crumble the matzah.
If they can do all of these things, then the feast is
a gift from Heaven. When they return to their
home, everything is exactly the same—except that
the magician is gone. They happily celebrate the
holiday.*

If only Elijah the Prophet could come here to the Warsaw Ghetto ...

Bubbie, you acted like a magician, a kishef-makher, the way you prepared for Shabes! Even in the Ghetto, you managed to make a tasty kugel with potato peels and a bit of an onion or carrot. When we had no candles or matches to light them, you said the prayer for them using two sticks when the sun went down, moving your hands in circles in front of your closed eyes. You insisted that we clean ourselves as best as we could every day—not just for Shabes.

Your fingers sewed white shrouds for the Burial Society of Warsaw. You carried your own shroud with you when the Nazis came and forced us out of our house. That one burial shroud somehow became three. Zayde cut and shaped each one, leaving holes so you could cling to each other by the hand, tying knots with threads over his tears.

In the hem of his trousers, he carries a picture of the Rosenfeld family taken before the war. We are all standing in Saski Park. Whenever he has a little extra thread, he is always reinforcing the stitches. We pray the picture will not be discovered and stolen from us.

He still wears a bandage over his face to cover the deep wounds. He looks strange to me; it is hard to get used to him without his beard. Mama, Papa, and Bubbie, you wouldn't recognize him at first. But you would know him by his soul. The Nazis can't change our insides. We won't let them.

We have grown so skinny from living in the Ghetto. Bread crossed our lips much more often four months ago, before we had to move here. At least we were all together. Like a flash, I can see a portrait of the Rosenfeld family in my mind. Mama, Papa, and Bubbie were alive then. Their bodies were not yet ravaged by the typhus that stole the lives of so many in the Ghetto.

But some memories are too hard to bear, and I push thoughts of my family away. The hurt in my heart remains, and I bite my lip to stifle my sobs. I don't wish to awaken the others.

It is very cold but my hand moving with this pen across these pages feels warm. The moonlight seeps through the window shade. I lift it carefully and struggle to see the words I have already written. My words call out to me from Hans Christian Andersen's story "The Steadfast Tin Soldier." Last time, I wrote in between the lines of "The Tinderbox." There are only eleven more stories. What will I do when I run out of paper?

I hold up this book and peer into it as though I am looking into a mirror.

I haven't seen a real mirror in a long time, but sometimes, when the watery soup is dished out at the children's kitchen at Nowolipki 68, I peer at my reflection. My eyes have grown wider and sharper somehow. They seem to pierce the bowl I carry in my hands. The soup gets stuck in my throat but I force it down.

I steal a look at my reflection while passing some of the shop windows on Karmelicki Street. Some of the bakeries set their wares right out front where we salivate so much that we nearly choke. I've seen little children break the windows and run off with rolls or cakes. They were starving. I know how they must have felt to do it. I pull myself away from those shop windows that sell food. It is the hardest thing I must do. Beggar children stand on the corner holding out their skinny hands, and well-dressed adults pass them by.

"Why?" Sorele would ask Zayde. But now, she too, has become so used to it that she no longer asks. But I mustn't think of food. I mustn't write about food. I must write of other things. Even now, although it is very late, I can hear the moans of beggars outside of this synagogue.

I know that many of them are children. Perhaps I have given books to some of them. Do they think of me with gladness the way I think of Batya? I remember the time she brought books to us when we needed them so desperately—when Mama, Papa, and Bubbie were dying. I didn't realize it then, but those few books that had given us so much pleasure were later collected and burned.

I am very happy to help Batya work with the children. She reminds me that I am also a child, but I do not feel like one. Since the bombs fell on Warsaw almost a year and a half ago, I feel like I have aged a thousand years, even though I am only twelve. My birthday was in September, just after the Germans invaded our land and the bombs fell. I was grateful to Batya then. She kept the Central Library open, and I walked there with Tsipoyre and Sorele to look at picture books. There was always a group of children gathered in the children's area. All of us had to step around the stone and rubble of fallen buildings to come. At least there was some place to go.

Batya read to us from her big book of fairytales. One story I especially loved was "The Wild Swans" by Hans Christian Andersen. I have the same story in my book. I asked Batya for this story again and again until she finally found a book written by Hans Christian Andersen. I wished to take it out so many times that one day, before we moved into the Ghetto, Batya told me I didn't need to bring it back to the library. Since then, this book has become my diary and my dear, familiar friend. I pause for a moment to kiss the page I am writing on.

The little girl in the story, Elisa, had to sew sweaters for her swan brothers to wear so that the spell placed upon them by their evil stepmother would no longer have any power over them. During the day, her brothers turn into swans and must fly, but during the night, until the dawn breaks, they are transformed into men again. Elisa must sew with prickly flax that burns her fingers but still she keeps on. And without a word. If she speaks a word, her work is all in vain.

Finally, just before she is to be killed for being a sorceress, Elisa throws the sweaters that she has made for her twelve swan brothers up into the sky. Miraculously, her swan brothers slip them on and turn into men again, except for the youngest brother who goes about with half a wing, for Elisa hadn't enough flax to sew him a whole sleeve. The crowd

gathered for her execution is certain that the
transformation they have witnessed is a sign from
Heaven that Elisa is innocent, and they free her.

But now the cries of beggar children pierce my thoughts and bring me back to this Ghetto ...

Once, we were free too, but when the Nazis came to Poland, we had to leave our apartment at Krolewska Street 24 and move here to the Ghetto. We had to leave our school, our teachers, and our friends. Halina and Szamek and their little daughter, Luba, came upstairs and gave us loaves of bread to take with us and promised we would see them again, but I don't think we ever shall.

My best friend, Maria, said goodbye to me outside of Saski Park. She told me that since it was forbidden for Jews to enter that park, she couldn't bring herself to go in either. But I said that she must go there whenever she could and think of me. If she thought of me hard enough while she sat under the trees in the sunlight, then maybe I could be there too — in spirit.

Now Polish people are living in our apartment. I picture the ivy overflowing in pots on our windowsill. We had to leave the plants behind. Is anyone watering them?

In the spring and summer, we all used to sit and watch people passing by as the white curtains gently danced with the breezes. Is anyone sitting on our wooden chairs now? Is it as cold on the Aryan side as it is in the Jewish Ghetto? We have no wooden chairs here — they have all been burned as firewood.

We are only a few blocks away from our friends but we may as well be across the world. So much hate like a great ocean separates us.

The Nazis even wish to separate us from our God. But this they cannot do, even though the synagogues are no longer houses of prayer since that is forbidden. People find ways to pray in all sorts of places, but even the synagogues have become apartments, like the one we live in.

I go with Batya to the synagogue on Tlomackie Street where there are three families living in the small sanctuary. Batya knocks softly. She calls out our names right away in Yiddish so no one will be frightened.

It is colder inside than outside. The children don't move at all from under their dirty covers—only their eyes follow us. We bring books and groats—the hot oatmeal—and when they see the food, out come their hands from under the covers, holding onto the bowls or cups that they always have with them.

We serve them with shivering spoons, and after they eat, we take out the books from our briefcases. I notice that the table the Torah once rested upon is now covered with personal articles—a comb, a brush, a piece of soap, a pair of socks, a towel. When I see a child's doll, I think of Sorele. The ark for the Torah serves as a cupboard now. Someone has placed a pile of armbands there like an offering.

I remember when the Torah from our Nowolipki Street synagogue was stolen by the Nazis and unraveled. Jews were forced to walk in the mud and then tread upon it. Even Grandfather had to step upon it. Anyone who refused to do this, the German soldiers shot on the spot.

Dear God, I think. Do You recognize Your house? It is as if You are no longer home. But surely You know Your people by their Jewish stars?

The children shed their dirty blankets and are drawn to the pictures on the covers of books. There are castles and magic wands. There are goats, sheep, and chickens on a farm. There are children laughing on a merry-go-round.

I guess that most of the children are between three and six. One of the older children is about seven or eight. His eyes are very big in his hollow face when he asks us to tell a story. My teeth are chattering but I begin "The Wild Swans" by Hans Christian Andersen. My voice gets stronger and stronger as I see the pictures in my mind.

> *"Far, far away, where the swallows fly when we have winter, there lived a King who had eleven sons and one daughter, Elisa. The eleven brothers, Princes all, each went to school with a star at his breast and a sword at his side. They wrote with pencils of diamond upon golden slates, and could say their lesson by heart just as easily as they could read it from the book. You could tell at a glance how princely they were. Their sister, Elisa, sat on a little footstool of flawless glass. She had a picture book that had cost half a kingdom …"*

It is the first time that I have told this story and I feel as though I have woven a magic spell. Even the mothers who are lying down near the pool of ice where a sewage pipe has burst, sit up and listen to me.

We leave the pile of books for them and explain we'll come back in two weeks to take them away and bring other books. The boy who wished for a story asks me for a book with "The Wild Swans" in it, and I must watch his face fall as I tell him that it is not in our pile today.

"Please come next time and tell it again," he says, looking at me with pleading eyes.

I nod as I pick up one of the empty briefcases. Batya picks up the other briefcase, along with the empty bowl of groats and the spoons.

Outside, on the steps of the synagogue, Batya calls for me to wait. She points to the window where the children and mothers wave at us and smile. I wonder at the sudden light in their eyes.

We walk in silence until we get to Leszno Street 67. The two adjoining rooms are cheerful with the cut-outs of paper dolls on the walls and toys and dolls on the bookshelves. This is the headquarters for the children's library. Many children's books in Polish and Yiddish are hidden here on the other side of the bookshelves.

We put down the briefcases and the big bowl with the spoons.

"It has been wonderful to have you work with me this past week," she says. "The whole Ghetto is blessed to have you share books and stories with these children,

Rivke. You bring some sort of magic — the way you share stories; the way you share books."

She opens up a drawer in one of the shelves and pulls out a pen.

"This pen is a gift. I wish I had some paper to give you, but it is very scarce, and I just have some old envelopes. I know you will find a way to write. And, after the war ..."

But she has to swallow and cannot finish her sentence, and I am so overwhelmed that I cannot speak.

I put the pen in the pocket of my coat and smile my thanks to her. I am crying because I am so happy. Someday I will remind her that she gave me the Hans Christian Andersen book that serves as my diary and my inspiration. All through the day, I am capturing memories in my mind so that I can write about them. I walk around with a happiness that makes me think of the rippling sunlight on the Vistula River.

But now the cries of beggar children puncture my ears the way that the sharp nettles made Elisa's fingers bleed in "The Wild Swans."

Dear God, I pray, would you allow me to sleep? Could you silence the mournful cries that hang in the night air like stones?

27 January 1941

IT IS SO cold in the morning that it hurts to breathe. Sorele, Tsipoyre, and I barely speak as we walk quickly to Nowolipki 68. I pull up my collar to help me keep out the cold. My brown hair twirls in all directions and so does Tsipoyre's long black hair and Sorele's brown curls. Thank God that our coats come down over our dresses and that we each have boots and Zayde's gifts of white scarves trimmed with blue. I think of my grandfather pushing his cart along Gesia Street and shivering there with the other street peddlers.

I think of him shuckling back and forth on the icy floor of the room in the synagogue at Nowolipki 27 where we live. He knows his prayers by heart — the way that I know Hans Christian Andersen's stories. In my mind, I can see the fringes of his tallis, his prayer shawl, dangling under his blanket. They remind me of the threads hanging from the torn coat of the Peddler of Wind.

Every day Zayde says Kaddish, the prayer for the dead, for Bubbie, Mama, and Papa. On Shabes, he does not touch his needle all day and prays with a group of men in the cellar of an apartment on Leszno Street, not far from the children's library. He takes us with him, and we sit with the women on the other side of the room. Throughout the service, someone always stands outside the door on the look-out for German soldiers. There is singing, and we all love that part, especially Tsipoyre. She closes her eyes and sways with her whole body, but her lips are sealed. Someday her lips will move with the words of the songs.

On Shabes, Zayde tells us stories from the Torah. I love to hear about Joseph who was sold into slavery by his brothers. He knows about the language of dreams and helps all of Egypt survive the terrible famine by telling the Pharaoh to set aside grain during the seven good years.

In the Ghetto, we would starve altogether if it weren't for the smugglers. Food comes to us from the other side of the wall—even in the carts used to pick up bodies for burial. I think of Gittel and Ruchel gathering food on the Other Side. I hope they are alright.

We pass two corpses wrapped in rags and newspapers as we walk to Nowolipki 68. They have frozen to death like the little match girl. We barely glance at them a second time since it is such a common sight. A beggar is already at work, stealing their rags and worn out shoes.

When we reach Nowolipki 68, we run up the stairs to the second floor where Estera greets us with a smile. We take off our coats and hang them on hooks in the hallway. It is warm in the kitchen because of the hot oatmeal on the stove and the kettles of water boiling. My eyes watch the squiggly lines of steam rise up into the air.

We hear crying at the bottom of the steps and Estera disappears quickly, returning with a little girl in her arms who is covered with rags. Her feet are purple with the cold. Her older brother follows Estera into the bright room — his own feet slipping out of shoes with holes.

Other children from nearby houses join us. Their tattered rags and coats hang next to our own. We all sit down at the table and hold our bowls of oatmeal tightly as if trying to extract warmth from them.

Estera welcomes everyone in Yiddish with "Sholem Aleykhem!" Most of us eat very quickly because we are so hungry and cold; Estera gently reminds us to slow down.

I find my way to the children who are looking out of the window. They are talking about the bodies they have seen lying in the street.

I want to tell them the story of "The Little Match Girl." It is a strange thing that I am standing next to two children at the window before I begin the story and when I am finished, I am sitting on the rug with all of the children and Estera gathered around me. I notice Tsipoyre hugging Sorele against her chest while Sorele is hugging her doll Margarita.

Then I see a new face looking at me. It is a woman with a big smile.

Estera breaks the silence and introduces the woman to us. "This is Gela Seksztajn," she says. "She is an artist and will show you some of her paintings. Then you will create your own."

Gela looks at me and asks me my name.

"Rivke Rosenfeld," I say.

"Rivke — first of all, thank you for your story. I am so glad that I was able to hear you tell it."

Then she holds up painting after painting of street scenes in the Ghetto. Each painting is filled with warm, bright colors — red, blue, purple, orange, yellow.

"The sky is very important," Gela explains. "I always look at the different colors in the sky. Sometimes it appears to be a dark, dismal day, but far off, beyond the clouds, there is always a streak of color — of light, of hope. I search for this and I paint it. And I try to feel the colors I have inside of my heart. I coax them out with my paintbrush and canvas."

And then, in front of us, she paints a picture of a little girl with a black tattered shawl wrapped about her shoulders, her hair blowing in the wind, her feet bare. In her hands, she holds a lit match, and the colors around it are pink and blue and violet.

"What do you think she is seeing in her imagination?" Gela asks us.

Estera writes down what the children say.

"Her mother. Her father. Her old house. Her school. Her grandmother. Bread. A rose. Bread. A cake ..."

Gela hands out a paintbrush to each of us. Estera places a piece of paper on the table near each child. Gela distributes the watercolors and some cups of water so we can clean off our paintbrushes.

"Paint the visions of the little match girl," she says. "Don't forget to think about the colors in the sky and the colors inside of your heart ready to come out."

We are all so busy. Gela and Estera walk softly among

us for encouragement. Estera catches our thoughts with her pen. All of the pictures are a swirl of color, and I think they are beautiful.

Gela smiles and asks if she can come back to visit us again and draw our portraits. "I am gathering a collection of children's faces from the Ghetto," she says.

She packs up her paintbrushes, paintings, and pieces of paper in her briefcase and gets ready to leave.

My eyes are still dizzy with the color she has brought to us. She must have smuggled the paints over the wall somehow.

We hug her, and she returns our hugs, unmindful of our stained fingers covered with paint.

On the way home, Tsipoyre, Sorele, and I hold hands and fill our eyes with the blue and white colors of the sky. The colors are like those of my armband with the Jewish star. I imagine I see all kinds of birds. There are eagles, sparrows, crows, swans, and geese. I raise my arms up high. Tsipoyre and Sorele look at me, a bit puzzled. They think I am playing. But I tell them very seriously that I am flying.

6 February 1941

FOR THE FIRST time, I am writing in the early morning light. I will write fast and furiously so as to finish before the others awaken.

I think of Hans Christian Andersen writing his stories. He was very poor, and when he became an adult, his stories made him rich and famous. What would he think if he knew that a young girl in the Warsaw Ghetto wrote her own words in between his own? So far, I have written in "The Steadfast Tin Soldier," "The Tinderbox," and "The Snow Queen." There are ten more stories. I am amazed that my words are clear, even though I have been writing in the dark.

Here is my memory and here is my story:

It is mid-afternoon. I am standing next to Sorele and Tsipoyre behind Zayde's cart on the crowded Ghetto street. We hold up some armbands with the Jewish stars. Since everyone aged twelve or older is required to wear an armband on their coats as well as on their sleeves underneath, this is a sure way to earn some zloty. The armbands mustn't be dirty or wrinkled. If a Jew is caught without one, he could be shot like Gittel and Ruchel's parents.

On one side of us, Mr. Tuchman is selling his books, and on the other side, Mrs. Rotstejn is selling her potatoes, holding them in her apron and in her hands.

It's cold and I'm hungry. People pass by in a hurry as though trying to escape the biting wind. A young woman with a deep frown is carrying a child. They pause in front of Zayde's cart. The little boy, wrapped in a dirty blanket, is laughing at Sorele's doll, Margarita, whose dress billows so much it looks like she is dancing. He points and gurgles and jumps up and down in his mother's arms. Sorele, Zayde, the young mother, and I all laugh. The mother passes us with a smile still on her face, her arms containing her bouncing son.

Then the Peddler of Wind limps towards us. I ask him: "What do you have in your sack? Wind?"

His glove puppet with its cocked hat, beard, and button eyes reaches into his little sack. "I carry wind wishes," he says in a soft voice.

"Do you have any fairytale wind?" I wonder aloud.

Suddenly, it is so windy that Sorele's doll is almost whisked from her hands and she starts to cry. Even the Peddler of Wind has to stop moving his hand with the puppet and pushes it instead into an opening of his coat, since he has no pockets. Zayde presses down on the armbands so that they won't blow away. Tsipoyre and I help him. In my mind, I see stars from the sky and feathers from birds. One little pillow flies up into the sky and disappears. So I start telling Sorele a story. I'm telling it for her sake as well as my own. And the gray day fades along with my hunger behind my words. I know

that Tsipoyre, with her arms hugging her coat around
her, and Zayde, with his fists curled into his pockets, are
listening, too. The Peddler of Wind stands as still as a
statue.

"Sorele," I say, and take her hand. She stops crying.
I begin my story.

*Once upon a time, in a Polish village near the
Vistula River, there was a little boy whose dream
it was to blow the shofar on Rosh HaShanah.
The rabbi gave him the shofar to practice blowing
during the Hebrew month of Elul, and he blew it
across the wide open fields near his home. It
seemed to the boy that whenever the tall grasses
swayed, and beyond them, he could see the
shimmering waters of the river, the wind surely
carried the sound of the shofar across the world.*

*When the boy blew the shofar, the geese
honked from the blue sky above and settled in the
field, sucking the dew from the grasses. Then all
was quiet as the boy watched them. He knew he
could summon the geese by bringing the shofar to
his lips, and this knowledge made him feel full of
awe. His grandfather would pray outside, his tallis
covering his head and shoulders. As he moved back
and forth, back and forth with the prayers, his
tallis rose up on either side of him, so that the boy
imagined that his grandfather became a great
goose flying with his feathers and his fringes. While
the grandfather prayed, the geese allowed the boy*

to stroke their feathers, and they would let him
walk among them in the tall, swaying grasses.

One goose stood above all the others and
anxiously looked upwards. One by one, the rest fell
into formation behind it, and then, after flapping
and jumping, they rose higher and higher, up from
the ground into the sky, their wings moving with a
great wind. The boy and his grandfather watched
them silently, and when the geese had gone, went
to comb the wide field for the gleaming white
feathers that they left behind in flight.

The boy would go with his grandfather to the
market, riding in the cart that their horse pulled
along. All during the month of Elul, the boy took
his shofar with him and blew it across the fields
and forests as he and his grandfather passed by.
The geese would respond with their own cries.

It was a strange and wonderful thing, the
villagers said, that the wild geese followed the two
of them as they made the journey to town and
hovered over them as they stood in the
marketplace. The grandfather bought cloth with
which to sew pillows that he stuffed with feathers
gathered from the wild geese. No longer did he
have to cut and sew patterns of trousers or jackets;
no longer did he have to sew buttons on coats or
hems on dresses. The pillows garnered a high price,
for never had the villagers rested their heads upon
anything that was so soft; never had the villagers
slept so well, even though sickness, worry, or fright

*plagued them during the daylight hours. There
were those who had no money with which to buy
pillows, and they would give the grandfather
bushels of apples, potatoes, or containers of honey.
There were those who had no money and nothing
to trade, but they would go to the marketplace just
the same to look at the geese that hovered in the air
near the boy and his grandfather.*

*The boy blew so clearly that word spread, and
it happened on Rosh HaShanah that many people
—Jews and non-Jews alike—came from miles
around to hear him blow the shofar in the little
wooden synagogue not far from the river. And
geese came from all over the countryside when they
heard him. They gathered quietly and sucked the
dew from the grasses that grew near the synagogue.
After the singing prayers, the geese flew away, and
children saved the white feathers and dreamed of
following the wild geese up into the sky.*

*At the end of Yom Kippur, the congregation
followed the boy outside to the field where he blew
the shofar for the last time. The geese cried out in
unison and then they flew away. No longer did the
geese follow the boy and his grandfather to the
marketplace now that the weather was becoming
colder. Occasionally, someone would wordlessly
point to his neighbor as a flock of wild geese flew
by overhead.*

*The boy gave the shofar back to the rabbi and
longed for the month of Elul when he would be*

*able to lift it to his lips once again. And so the
years passed.*

*When the boy was twelve and his grandfather
was ninety-six, strange soldiers with twisted crosses
on their uniforms invaded Poland and bombs fell
on the land. People were afraid to walk outside
and geese were afraid to fly down to the ground.*

*One day, the Jews of their village were told
to gather in the main square at an appointed time
with their most precious belongings in sacks. People
frantically packed their bundles and set off for
the main square, pushing carts or wheelbarrows,
or carrying their bundles on their backs as they
walked. The adults took some clothes, some food,
some pots and pans, their photographs, their books.
The children took some clothes and their toys—a
truck, a doll, a book. The boy and his grandfather
took some clothes and all of the pillows that they
could stuff into their sacks.*

*When the rabbi was packing up ritual objects
from the old wooden synagogue, he came upon the
shofar that the boy loved to blow. The rabbi made
his way through the crowd of people waiting in the
main square with their bags and bundles to learn
of their fate. He found the boy and his grandfather
wrapped under the grandfather's tallis. They were
praying together. The rabbi hated to interrupt
their prayers but knew he had to do so. He quickly
slipped the shofar from his bag of ritual objects to
the sack of pillows that the boy and his grandfather*

*were sitting upon. Pretending to arrange the items
in the sack of pillows, the boy reached for the shofar
and blew it softly. Almost instantly, wild geese
silently rose in the sky and swirled above the heads
of the Jews. It was as if they were saying goodbye.*

*Then all of the Jews were put on trains that
stank from the sweat of cattle. Many hours later,
they arrived in the Warsaw Ghetto. When they
arrived, their clothes were soiled, their mouths
were dry, and their spirits were low. They stood
up straight and tall, however, when they noticed
a few of the wild geese flapping their tired wings
above them. Then those strange soldiers with
twisted crosses on their uniforms threw stones at
some of the geese and shouted sharply at them.
The geese honked loudly and flew away.*

*Although they arrived in the Ghetto during
the month of Elul, the boy was afraid to practice
blowing the shofar. It was too dangerous to be seen
or heard with such a Jewish object.*

*On the eve of Rosh HaShanah, the boy missed
the sound of the shofar so much that he reached
into the sack of pillows and pulled it out gently. He
touched it with his hands. Word traveled through
the Ghetto that there was to be a special children's
service that evening in honor of the holiday. Quietly,
families arrived in the apartment building near a
small courtyard. When everyone had gathered in
the designated room, especially those from the village
of Pinczow, the grandfather placed a blanket over*

the door and closed it as tightly as he could. The rabbi said some prayers in a hushed voice and then turned to the boy who knew it was time to blow the shofar. He blew it slowly, unsure of the sound that would be heard. He lowered it from his lips and listened for the sound of the beating feathers of wild geese. He waited, but no geese came to the Ghetto. Then the boy put down the shofar, handed it to his grandfather, and rushed out of the room.

Where did he go? No one moved.

The boy returned with his sack filled with pillows. Motioning for the congregation to watch him, he stepped outside into the small courtyard. He ripped open each of the pillows and the many feathers slid to the ground. Then the boy came back into the room, and he placed the blanket over the door once again. He picked up the shofar from his grandfather's hands and he began to blow— softly at first and then steadily louder. The people became afraid. "Stop!" they whispered hoarsely. "Someone will hear and discover us!"

Finally, the boy lowered the shofar from his lips and closed his eyes. His face was attentive as though he was listening for something far away. Then he carefully slipped the blanket away from the door and opened it. A glimpse of white, gleaming, rustling feathers made the congregation catch their breath. In that courtyard barren of grasses, wild geese stood proudly against the night. People were

*so happy to see them that they went outside and
hugged them like they were old relatives.*

*Shedding silent tears, the boy took his armband
with the Star of David off of his coat and stuck it
in the feathers of one of the geese. The others followed
his example.*

Suddenly, heavy footsteps could be heard.

*Quickly, without making a sound, the geese
and the small congregation went back into the
room with the door that they had sealed and closed
off with a blanket. Not a single child cried and
not a single goose honked. It was a miracle that
they all managed to fit inside. They stood, cramped
in that room, barely breathing, until the heavy
footsteps passed. Then the children led the geese
outside, but they would not fly away.*

*"Go! You must! It isn't safe to be a Jew here!"
they whispered.*

*The children tried to coax the geese to leave by
flapping their arms like pretend wings. But the geese
did not move. The boy blew a short soft sound on
the shofar to encourage them to fly away.*

*Then the bright white feathers brought
unwanted attention, and the patrolling German
soldiers found the congregation in the midst of the
geese in the courtyard. The belt buckles of the
Germans glistened almost as much as the feathers.*

*"Where are your stars?" the soldiers asked the
group, pointing to their elbows that were devoid
of armbands.*

The boy pointed to the geese. The soldiers sneered at the Jews standing before them when they noticed the armbands attached to the feathers of the geese. One of the soldiers slowly pulled back his gun and aimed it at one of the geese. At that moment, the boy raised the shofar to his lips and blew it with all of the wind he had inside of him. The geese cried out with their haunted cries and fluttered their wings so powerfully that dust and dirt and the horrible smell of human waste blew into the faces of the German soldiers. The soldier holding up his gun fired a few random shots and then dropped the weapon because he couldn't see.

A few seconds later, the air was miraculously still and all was silent. The geese and the Jews from the courtyard were gone. The wide-eyed soldiers sucked in their breath, took off their helmets, and bowed their heads. On the ground were wrinkled armbands with the Star of David and a few gleaming white feathers that had dropped in flight.

I get lost in my words. Sorele is still standing beside me, but I'm no longer holding her hand. Tsipoyre looks up at the sky.

Zayde looks at me from dark shadows under his eyes. He is asking me "is it true?" with his whole face. That is what everyone is asking me with their faces. I've been telling my story to a half circle of people standing around Zayde's cart. The Peddler of Wind, the woman selling apples, the people who have just bought potatoes from the man with the cart across the street, the beggar children who must have come to listen to my story after following the Balloon Man.

I see a man wearing a cross around his neck but an armband above his elbow. Even though he tries so hard to be a Christian, the Nazis never let him forget that he was born a Jew. Maybe he is on his way to the church on Leszno Street. Before he passes by, he comes right up to me. His glasses are clouded from the snow.

"Thank you," he says to me, and bows slightly. I do not say anything—I can only smile from under my scarf. He pauses a moment and looks at the pillows in the cart. He points to one and pays Zayde. I think to myself that now he will have Jewish dreams whether he wants to or not.

I recognize the two patrolling German soldiers who stole the beard from my grandfather's face. Their eyes have a faraway look in them—not the cold, mean, piercing gaze of hate like when I saw them before. It's on account of the story, I know. Their souls are hungry for stories, too.

They are leaning against one of the pushcarts, thumbs hooked against their belt loops. The magic of my story makes me bold and I hold my head up to meet their eyes directly. First one of them pulls his helmet down over his eyes and then the other one does the same thing. They walk away quietly as if they have no wish to disturb us.

The wind sweeps across the street, and I can hear a

child crying in the distance. I think of the cries of the wild geese from my story. The hollow faces around Zayde's cart come closer to me.

I notice the Peddler of Wind looking at me behind his thick black eyebrows and beard. His little puppet holds something up to its mouth and blows. It is a shofar. The puppet becomes the boy in my story. And then the puppeteer's hands become the wings of a bird. One of the Jewish geese. He walks past Zayde's cart with his hands moving up and down like that. The children gathered around the cart follow him wordlessly the way I have seen them follow the Balloon Man.

Mrs. Rotstejn bends over in the snow to pick up her potatoes. She has been listening so hard she must have dropped them!

Gela Seksztajn comes up to me and touches my face with her gloved hands. She has bought a pair from Zayde —I recognize his blue and white scraps. I feel my frozen cheeks thaw as she cups them in her hands.

"Rivke Rosenfeld. I would love to paint your portrait. You have the face of an artist, a kinstler. Your story needs to be told again and again. Soon, I will visit the kitchen at Nowolipki 68, and perhaps you can sit for me then."

I nod as she pats my face gently. Then she turns and walks away, her blue scarf dancing in the wind.

"Rivke," I hear someone say behind me. I turn around and see Mrs. Tuchman.

"Your story makes me stronger. I know these bunches of rags that you call 'pillows' don't have any feathers inside of them, but I will be hoping that just maybe, it is possibly true. And so I will buy two. One for me and one for my husband. We will sleep better even though we are living in such madness." And she reaches over and hands me three zloty from her pocket. I choose two pillows and give them to her. She touches them tenderly.

Others come close to me and place zloty in my hand, and I give them to Tsipoyre. People hold the pillows that they buy close to themselves as though they carry some sort of magic.

Then I turn and there are only five pillows left in the cart! There were forty before.

Sorele looks up at me with pride.

"Zayde! Look!" Sorele cries. "Rivke sold almost all of the pillows!"

Zayde hugs me to him and I can feel the tears on his cheeks.

"You make me believe that my little steel needle is made of gold and my little rag pillows are stuffed instead with feathers of wild geese. You make me grateful for your stories. You carry the gift within you through these dark, terrible days. Hold onto your stories, Rivke! Remember them! We all need to hear them."

I am warmed by his words, but it is the face of one of the beggar children that I can still see in my mind. I recognize him from my visit to the synagogue on Tlomackie Street. He is the child who wished for a book with the story "The Wild Swans." He comes up to me with a grosz that he holds in his dirty hand. "Please," he says. "I'd like to buy a pillow."

I have seen him near the wall carrying bundles in his arms and under the sleeves of his coat. He is a smuggler. I know that the bundles must be loaves of bread and sacks of potatoes. But he looks so skinny. I want to give him a hug and say: "Be careful!"

Of course, I could not take his coin. "I have an extra one," I say. "You can have it."

I give him a pillow. His eyes light up.

"I am the one you were speaking about in the story. My name is Shmuel. I come from the village of Pinczow, and I love to blow the shofar, too. I believe that geese came in the story, and they will come here. In the Ghetto. I will pray for them to come."

I marvel at the effect my story has had on so many people. I pick up a pillow and squeeze it.

Then I notice Batya talking with Mr. Tuchman. He hands her a pile of books that she stuffs into her briefcase. I know that these are the children's books he has set aside for her to take to the library. Some of them are taped up. Is this because the cruel German soldier ripped them?

Batya beckons me over to her. She is standing some distance away from the carts and all the foot traffic. Zayde, Tsipoyre, and Sorele are busy selling armbands. My story brings many people to Zayde's cart and they linger there.

Batya's face is shining as she introduces me to a tall man with dark hair who shakes my hand warmly.

"This is Rivke Rosenfeld," Batya says. "The storyteller—the one I was telling you about."

She tells me his name is Dr. Emanuel Ringelblum. I think I have met his son, Uri, who is about Tsipoyre's age.

In a low voice, Dr. Ringelblum tells me that he is in charge of a group that is gathering all kinds of documents pertaining to life in the Ghetto.

"Your story is too valuable to be lost!" he says. "You have a gift." He wants to know if I would be willing to write down my story and my memories so that they could become part of the Warsaw Ghetto Archive. Eventually, all of the collected materials will be carefully buried in a secret underground place, away from the eyes of the Nazis, who would surely destroy everything if they found it.

He wants to know if I would please not tell anyone about this conversation, and would I please consider doing what he asks of me.

I nod and his eyes shift to Batya who has been listening quietly.

"Batya—could you possibly find some paper for her?"

"I already have been writing in the old library book of Hans Christian Andersen stories Batya has given me, and I have also been writing with the pen she has given me."

Dr. Ringelblum looks at Batya and then at me. They both look surprised and then delighted.

Batya exclaims: "You must write the story out and Gela can illustrate it, Rivke! Then we can put your book in our library and it will be available to borrow!"

I imagine my story in between the pages of a book and my heart begins to flutter. I feel like I am dreaming when Dr. Ringelblum shakes my hand again, pumping it up and down.

"Rivke Rosenfeld—thank you so much for your desire to contribute to the Underground Archive. Thank you especially for your story. We will speak again."

And then, an amazing thing happens.

"Rivke," he says. "I would like to buy that pillow."

I look down. I have forgotten that I am still holding it in my hand.

He pulls out a bill from his pocket, and I offer him the pillow.

Batya kisses me on the forehead. "My famous story-teller," she whispers. "My budding librarian. Keep writing."

The two of them turn and walk away, speaking intensely under their breath.

I stand on the other side of the street in a daze.

Sorele runs over to me and pulls my hand in the direction of Zayde and Tsipoyre. She is so excited she can hardly contain herself.

"Rivke! All of the armbands are sold, too!"

Zayde hugs me again, and I give him the money I still have in my hand. It is ten zloty!

Tsipoyre pushes her long black hair away from her face and stares at me.

"Rivke—what is it that makes you tell a story like that?"

She is thinking about her wish to be able to sing again, and I must answer her carefully.

"Remember when those cruel soldiers stole Zayde's beard from him? Something happened inside of me then. I became very, very angry and decided that they will never take my soul, my spirit. They will never take my stories away. I will not let them. My stories are like your songs, Tsipoyre. We carry them deep inside, where no one can see them. And they can't take away what is invisible."

Tsipoyre opens her arms and enfolds me in a hug.

"No one can ever take the memory of that hug away from us," she says when she releases me.

I plant a kiss on her cheek and think about my conversation with Dr. Ringelblum. I am not the only one who dreams of planting words deep in the ground, away from the eyes of our enemies.

Oh, dear God! I want to live! I want to breathe fresh air, run through an open field, laugh loudly, eat until I feel full, and write without fear.

It is forbidden to pray in a synagogue or to blow a shofar. We are like trapped birds fluttering against the wall of this Ghetto. But in the night, I can hold a rag pillow under my head, and I will dream of wild geese.

In the night, I dream of the boy, Shmuel. He is grasping the pillow that reminds him of the story he believes in so fervently.

And then I glimpse the Peddler of Wind behind this boy. He is nodding his head slowly. His eyes are closed. His long gray beard flies over his shoulder. Doesn't he know it is dangerous to have such a long beard?

The hand holding the puppet is turning and twirling. The puppet seems to be alive and dancing. The Peddler of Wind's lips are moving but what is he saying? I seem to hear a song coming from far away. I speak to him in my dream.

"Would you give me some wind from your sack? Fairytale wind?"

He smiles a smile so wide that it covers his whole face. He opens his bright eyes and looks into my own, throwing me something with one hand. I touch what I catch in my fist. Wind. Wind that carries the smell of tall grasses, the light of the autumn sun, and the promise of wild geese in flight. My pockets are all torn, so I open my coat and put the handful of wind into the pocket of my heart.

"Thank you," I whisper to the Peddler of Wind. "A sheynem dank. Thank you very much."

I watch him as he limps away, his sack upon his back. His puppet looks like him, with its beard wrapped around its neck for warmth. I can hear him singing softly with each step.

"Broyt, broyt. A bisele broyt ..."

Or — is he crying?

I wake up in the night and see Gittel and Ruchel across the room combing their hair in the shadows. They comb with the same rhythm. First one side and then the other. It is like they are rowing. I wonder how many nights they have combed their hair like this while we have all been sleeping.

Very quietly and carefully, I step over the bodies of Zayde and my sisters until I am able to sit down near Gittel and Ruchel in the corner. My whispered words come out so quickly that I surprise even myself.

"You live on the Aryan side," I say. "You are smugglers. You pretend to be Polish."

I am glad to hear them answer me in Yiddish.

"You are right about us," Gittel says. "We pass on the Other Side. It's on account of our hair and our eyes. Our secret weapons. Outside of the Ghetto, we take off our armbands and pull out crosses from under our clothes. We become Teresa and Rosalia Kozlowski. My saint's feast day is October 15th. Ruchel's — Rosalia's — is September 4th. We must know these things, Rivke. We can say the 'Hail Mary,' the 'Our Father,' and other prayers, too."

They pull out their crosses and baptismal certificates that hang on strings around their necks. I gasp. My mouth and eyes open so wide that they both shush me by putting their fingers against my lips.

"You make me think of the Warsaw Mermaid, the Syrenka Warszawska," I say. "I remember how my friend Maria and I loved to sit near her on the banks of the Vistula River before the war. She holds a sword in one hand and a shield in the other — ready to protect us all."

I think to myself that there are so many stories told about the Syrenka Warszawska. Usually a fisherman captures her, and she pleads with him to be free. She is so grateful when he releases her that she guards the city of Warsaw forever after.

Maybe she is one of the sisters from "The Little Mermaid" story told in my book. I have just written in between the margins.

This is the story that I tell to Gittel and Ruchel.

*Once, there was a mermaid named Irena who
lived in the North Sea that surrounded Denmark.
She lived with her twin sister, Sofia, and every
morning they rose to the surface of the water to
sing. They sang so beautifully that many sailors
stopped to listen. More and more, Irena longed for
the beautiful world of trees, flowers, birds, and
people that she glimpsed as she sang with her sister
along the shore. One day, she could not sing at all
because she was so sad. That night, she visited the
old witch who lived at the very bottom of the sea,
and she spoke of her longing to walk with two legs
and live on the land. The old witch agreed to give
her a magic potion that would make her tail split
into two legs. The price was high—there would be
much pain every time she took a step, and she would
have to give up her lovely voice and her life in the
sea. Her sister, Sofia, begged her not to purchase
the potion from the old witch. "Be content with the
friendly fish, sea animals, and shimmering waves!"
Sofia said. "You can swim to the surface of the
water anytime you wish to sit on the rocks and sing.
Then you can have your fill of looking about you at
the wide world above the sea. Let this be enough!"*

*But as much as Sofia pleaded, Irena did not
listen. When the light from the stars twinkled over
the top of the water while Sofia slept, Irena swam
to the very bottom of the sea to meet the old witch.
Early the next morning, as the sun rose, she swam
to the surface of the water and drank the potion.*

Her tail split into two pink slender legs, and the pain was so great that she wanted to cry out. Her mouth opened wide, but she discovered that she had no voice, as the witch had warned her. She could not stop the flow of tears as she sat on the rocks and waited for her sister to find her. From time to time, Irena traveled from shore to distant shore with kind fishermen in their boats. She was so beautiful and so sad that they took pity upon her and tried hard to understand her gestures.

When Irena was nowhere to be found, Sofia became so worried about her that she swam to the old witch in her hut at the bottom of the sea.

"You have given her a potion that has granted her two legs but you have stolen her voice! Now she has lost her tail and cannot return to the sea! What can you do to reverse this curse?"

The old witch was afraid of the look she saw in the mermaid's eyes.

"I cannot reverse the curse," she said quietly, with the voice that had once been her sister's. "But I can give you a magic sword and shield that will allow you to protect your sister when you do find her."

The years passed. Sofia swam from the North Sea near Denmark and on to Sweden, searching desperately for Irena. She rested on rocks near the shore and sang about her sister—how much she missed her, how much she loved her, how much she wished to protect her with her sword and shield.

*The rushing waves grew quiet, and sailors stopped
their own singing to listen to Sofia. But just when
they thought they understood her songs, she swam
away to the Norwegian Sea and on to the Baltic
Sea. The Baltic Sea led her along the banks of the
Vistula River in Poland, where she paused to rest,
grasping her shield and brandishing her sword.
She sang about her sister so mournfully that the
people who lived in Warsaw near the flowing river
came close to listen. The Christians blessed her with
the sign of the cross, and the Jews blessed her with
Yiddish words. "Zay gezunt," they said. "Stay well
and keep well."*

*In time, Sofia stopped singing because her
sorrow was so great. She rested silently on the
banks of the Vistula, always with her sword and
shield poised. The people of Warsaw felt comforted
to see her there. The old told the young her story,
and whenever someone took the road in or out of
the city, they brought her food, drink, and
garments to keep her warm. They polished her
sword and shield so that it glistened in the sun,
and she was grateful.*

*When war came, the bombs fell and the
buildings crumbled, but Sofia held her sword
and shield more tightly, and her face was set in
a determined frown. She gave the people courage.
"We will be like the Syrenka Warszawska, the
Warsaw Mermaid, during this terrible time. She
is strong and brave," the people said to each other.*

*And when the Jews were herded into the
Warsaw Ghetto, Sofia began to cry. The tears that
slid down her face fell all the way to her shoulders,
and then wings the color of sea foam magically
sprouted from her shoulder blades.*

*Sometimes, in the darkness, she flies over the
wall of the Warsaw Ghetto, spreading her wings
very wide. She drops apples, potatoes, and loaves
of bread near starving people and then continues
on her way. She is still searching for her sister.
"Irena! Irena!" she calls, sounding like a great
bird. You can hear her at night in between the
cries of beggars. She rests when she can, holding
her body very still, like a statue, on the banks of
the Vistula River.*

Gittel and Ruchel hug each other tightly. "That is *our*
story! We will make it our own!"

Then they are out of breath. They tuck their crosses and baptismal certificates under their clothes.

"Rivke!" Ruchel says. "You are strong and brave to
make up such a story! Listen! Ask if your zayde can sew
the Syrenka Warszawska on pillows! We will smuggle
them to the Other Side! We will tell your story! Now we
must get ready to go across. Others will be expecting us."

I want to tell them about Zayde's pillows and "The
Jewish Geese" story but there is no time.

They slip on their armbands in one motion. Then
they both kiss me—one on one side and one on the other.
I grasp their hands and try to make my voice steady.

"May God watch over you, Gittel and Ruchel—Teresa and Rosalia."

And then they are gone.

I am aware of a deep sadness inside of my heart and let the tears spill out from my eyes. But I am as silent as Irena in the story. The Jews are like Irena. We have lost our voice though our tears may burn our faces. Will the world ever know of our sorrow?

11 February 1941

I AM AMAZED at the power of my story. Zayde has made a new design on a few of his pillows — flying geese with a Jewish armband on one outstretched wing. They are very popular. He has made enough money to even buy some feathers for stuffing a few of them.

I have told Zayde the Syrenka Warszawska story and about Gittel and Ruchel — Teresa and Rosalia. He has started to sew the Warsaw Mermaid designs on new pillows. When I look over at him sewing in the small sanctuary, he picks up his head and gestures to me with his curved finger. I kneel in front of him, and he holds my face in his hands.

"Tayere Rivke, dear Rivke! You are a marvel! Your stories make me feel like I am fighting against the Nazis by sewing with this little needle. Your parents would be so proud, so happy. May God watch over you!"

"Tayere Zayde," I say. "Tayere, tayere Zayde." We kiss each other's noses like we used to do when I was a little girl.

I watch him go back to his sewing. We will see how many pillows he can make before Gittel and Ruchel return

from the Other Side. I try to stay awake through the
night, hoping to see them. But I am just too tired.

Dr. Ringelblum visits Zayde's cart and buys three more
of the beautiful geese pillows. He shakes my hand warmly. "Now I will never forget your story!" he says.

In the library, Batya gives me four pieces of clean
white paper. "For your story," she says. "I have already
spoken to Gela. She is working on the illustrations." I
think of her using blue for the sky, green for the field.

Before Batya and I set out to bring books to the children, she shows me a copy of a secret Ghetto newspaper.
There is a picture of one of Zayde's pillows. The caption
under the drawing says: "Be strong! Have faith!" I look
at it for a long time. The words at the bottom of the sheet
of paper say: "Pass this along to a neighbor or friend. Do
not leave this paper lying around. If you are the last one
to read it, burn it."

On the street, as I walk with Batya, we pass rick-
shas powered by men who drag Jews along on seats on
wheels. Once, horses were the beasts of burden. Now
these young men sweat and groan under the strain of
their load. Jewish policemen walk by with their blue
coats, caps, and rubber batons. I watch how they yell for
the woman in front of us to show her work papers. She
can hardly speak, she is so frightened. The policemen
wave her papers in her face and yell some more. Beggars
cry and sing for bread. I wonder how there can be so
much shouting on one street.

Then beggar children approach us, waving and calling out our names. They seem to appear in every direction.

We arrive at an empty lot close to the Jewish cemetery, and I pause to touch the ground. It is very cold, but there is no snow. We spread out the blanket Batya carries in her knapsack, and everyone finds a place to sit.

I tell them the story I have recently read in a book of folktales from Japan about the young man who wishes for a wife. One day, he is out in the forest searching for wood to chop down. All the branches are covered with snow. He is about to return home when he notices a beautiful white crane, frozen with the cold. He blows his own breath for a long time on her wings until she can finally move them up and down and fly away. Late that night, there is a knock at his door. When he goes to open it, a beautiful woman wearing a white dress stands there, shivering from the cold. He invites her in and falls in love with her. They agree to marry, and even though they are very poor, they are very happy.

But the man, who is a woodcutter, becomes despondent because he wishes they had more money. His wife explains that she is a weaver. Since she has noticed a loom in the back room of the hut, she will use it to weave cloth for him that he may sell in the marketplace. "The only thing I ask of you is not to look in on me while I am weaving. I will come out when the cloth is ready."

The man worries about his wife, who stays inside of the room for such a long time. All the while, he can hear the constant whirring of the loom. Finally, she opens the door weakly and hands her husband the most beautiful cloth he has ever seen. It seems to glow with its own light.

The husband excitedly thanks her for the cloth, and then he takes a good look at her face. She is pale and there is sweat above her upper lip. He comes close and hugs her to him, asking why she has become so tired. She shakes her long black hair and only answers him with a wan smile.

The husband sells the cloth for a good price in the marketplace, and they live without worries for many months. But the time comes once again when he is despondent. There has been a heavy snowfall, and it is difficult to find dry wood to chop down. Meanwhile, the money from the cloth has been spent upon food. His wife explains that she will go into the little room and weave some more cloth that he will be able to sell in the marketplace. Then he will sell the cloth for a good price and will be happy.

This time, when his wife stays behind the closed door and works the loom, the husband becomes especially curious. She doesn't come out for three days, and all the while he can hear the constant whirring of the loom.

"Could anything be wrong? Why does she not come out? And why does she warn me not to look

in on her while she is weaving? I am her husband!
Surely I can open the door just a crack?"

The husband opens the door and is so shocked
by what he sees that he is frozen in place, his fingers
around the doorknob. There is the loom, and there
is a white luminous cloth in between the slats. But
where is his wife? He can see only a crane plucking
her own feathers from her bleeding chest.

"I am the crane you once warmed with your
own breath when my wings were frozen with the
cold. I came to you that night as a young woman
in gratitude. But now that you have seen me in
my crane form, I must leave you."

The man is so sad that he cries many tears
and they fall upon the feathers of the crane.

"I am sorry that I did not heed your warning!
I promise never to look upon you again while you
are weaving. I did not know that you would weave
your own feathers into the cloth!"

The crane looks at the man with great sorrow
in her eyes and drops the cloth into his lap. It is
even more beautiful than the other cloth — lighter
to the touch and more luminous.

Then the crane opens up the door to the little
hut with her wing and flies away. Her husband
watches her from the frosted windowpane until she
is out of sight.

The children are quiet after I tell the story. Then Batya and
I take out the books we have brought in the briefcases

and lay them on the blanket. The children reach for them.

I close my eyes and put my head down. I picture the crane pulling out her own feathers with her beak and weaving them into her cloth. How weak she became! Will I become weak, too?

I think of my own words that I pull up from deep within me, and I fall asleep.

When I wake up, the boy, Shmuel, is next to me, quietly looking at a book. Batya is reading to a small group of children. She is hugging them under her arms as she reads so that she cannot even move to turn the pages.

"I am watching over you," Shmuel says. "The way that the man watched over the crane when she was so cold."

This is the boy who came up to me with a grosz in his dirty hand, and I gave him a pillow without taking his coin. He looks at me intently.

"And now I will tell a story," he says. "It is called 'The Jewish Geese.' It is a true story. It happened in my village, and I pray it will happen here, in the Ghetto."

And as he tells my story, I listen so deeply that the hunger cramps in my stomach stop, and I don't feel the icy wind. His voice telling my story wraps me up in a magic spell. The story isn't mine any longer. I have given it away and have received a gift in return.

I close my eyes and picture the crane pulling out her own feathers with her beak and weaving them into her cloth. The feathers are my stories, and the glistening cloth is my diary.

I open my eyes and watch the way those Germans

walk our streets and guard our gates with their shiny belt buckles, well-fed paunches, and beady eyes, forever looking to catch us unawares. It makes me think there must be magic that we Jews carry in our pockets to rile them up so. Even the Jewish policemen guard us so vigorously! What if someday my words were buried right under the snow and stones that they kick away with their heavy boots?

As I look straight ahead, my eyes run into the barbed wire of the wall of this Ghetto. I look past the wire and try to see the color of the sky. I comb my mind for images of the sun and stars, clouds and rivers, trees, birds, and flowers, and these become the cornerstones of my stories. For if we can remember the beauty we once knew in the world, all is not lost, and we must try not to be afraid.

Here is my dream:

Shmuel motions for me to come close to him. "I know how to climb over the wall like a cat," he whispers. "I smuggle many loaves of bread and sacks of potatoes."

I want to ask him: "Do you know the Goldman sisters—Gittel and Ruchel?" But instead I say: "Be careful!" as I hug him quickly. He disappears over the wall in a flash.

I slip through a hole in the wall and Sorele, Tsipoyre, and Zayde follow me. Once we are on the Aryan side, Zayde and I take off our armbands. The sky is a grayish-black in the Ghetto and so are our clothes and our hair —everything is gray and ugly. On the Other Side, I cannot stop blinking. The sky is full of bright sunshine and white drifting clouds against the blueness.

Women walk past wearing orange and pink flowers on their skirts; children have on red and yellow hats. I see someone who looks just like Maria, with black braids clipped on the top of her head. But when she passes by, I see that it is not my friend. We are startled to hear our names and stop to turn around. Halina and Luba hurry towards us, waving and smiling. Halina carries Luba, and their brown hair has golden tints to it.

"Come! I want to show you something!" Halina says, with her face all aglow.

We follow her up the stairs into the building where we used to live. Shmuel is waiting for us. Inside of their apartment, Halina shows us a pillow. I take a good look. It is one of Zayde's pillows with the Jewish geese embroidered on it. Zayde turns it over and over in his hands. He looks puzzled.

"Don't you see?" Shmuel says to him. "They have flown to the Other Side."

13 February 1941

A STRANGE MEMORY:

I am walking back from the kitchen at Nowolipki 68 with Sorele and Tsipoyre. On the way, we hear beautiful music. We peek through a crack in the wall and glimpse children with coats, boots, gloves, and hats sitting on painted horses that go up and down. We stand there, transfixed at the sight of these children on a merry-go-round. The music is Chopin. I am reminded of how Halina used to play the piano for Luba, when she started to cry. As soon as Luba heard her mother play, she stopped her whimpering. I used to stand still in our apartment downstairs, bathed in sunlight, holding my breath as I listened. "He was a Polish composer," Halina once said to me of Chopin. "But his music is so beautiful, he belongs to the world."

Before we know it, a group of beggar children gathers around us. They are so surprised to see the purple horses.

An old Polish woman wearing a kerchief looks back at us from behind the crack of the wall. She smiles kindly, and I can see the wrinkles around her mouth and eyes. A moment later, she enters the Ghetto, first bribing a Polish guard who turns his head in the opposite direction as though he does not see her. From her bag, she pulls out scarves, hats, gloves. She pulls out apples, onions, and carrots and helps us stuff everything in our sleeves and pockets. Before we can thank her, she disappears.

We turn our attention again to the purple horses. I think about how I must ask Batya if she can find me a book about Pegasus, the Greek horse that had magic wings. I would like to tell this story to the children.

My fingers grasping this pen race across this page. I pray that my words will be clear enough to read but I cannot slow down.

I can hear the rise and fall of everyone breathing around me. That alone is a miracle. A few hours ago, our hearts stopped from the moyre, the fear.

This is what I remember:

I am sitting cross-legged on my mattress, wrapped in my blanket as I write. I am hearing merry-go-round music in my head. I am wondering if Gittel and Ruchel have ever seen the painted horses. I sit up straight to look at them sleeping on the other side of the room.

Suddenly, the sound of heavy boots punctures my thoughts. Soldiers are coming down the steps to our sanctuary! There is no lock anymore so they open the door and walk right in.

My pen becomes rigid and I cannot seem to close my book. I force myself to swallow my fear and I shove my book and pen inside of my pillow. I drop down to my straw mattress and bury myself in my blanket. I imagine myself flying away with invisible wings.

Two German soldiers wielding flashlights stomp into the room, and the floor shakes.

"Hände hoch, Juden!" one of them shouts. "Hands up, Jews!"

We all raise our heads and sit up. I am worried about Sorele. She rubs her eyes, but does not cry out. She holds up her hands above her head like the rest of us.

My eyes circle the room. Zayde, Tsipoyre, Gittel, and Ruchel all raise their hands and keep their heads down. Gittel and Ruchel quickly pull black scarves over their hair, but it peeks out anyway. Sorele raises her head with a frightened, puzzled look. I raise my head high because I feel bold. I look at the two soldiers directly as though I have nothing to hide.

The soldiers march towards each of us in turn. They shine their flashlights in our eyes and on our rags. Then one soldier leans against the wall and doesn't move. I call him Statue Man in my mind.

The other soldier comes close to Gittel, rips off her scarf, and strokes her wavy blonde hair. His hand travels down to the front of her coat and he reaches under it to touch her breasts. I hold my breath. What about her cross? What about her baptismal certificate? What can I do? But I feel as frozen as the Warsaw Mermaid statue near the Vistula River.

Gittel pulls back from the soldier. "Nein! Nein! —No! No!" The Yiddish is the same as the German. He slaps her across the face.

"Who is giving the orders here? Do you forget you could be shot in one second?"

She pulls the coat around herself and turns her face away. He sticks out his boot as though to kick her, but he does not. I call him Big Boot in my mind. He holds up his gun and then puts it down. Gittel and Ruchel do not move.

The soldier lets his flashlight linger on their identical faces and laughs. Then he moves it down to Ruchel's chest. The buttons on her coat go in and out with the beating of her heart.

Big Boot rips off her scarf and throws it down. He touches her breasts underneath her coat. I pray that he will not feel her wooden cross. Then he takes his hand away and covers his mouth as he yawns.

"I will see you beauties again when it is not so late, and I am not so tired. You remind me of my Inga, who once loved me."

Big Boot spots Zayde's cart against the wall. He picks it up and throws it upside down. It crashes to the floor and a wheel rolls off. It is empty, except for Zayde's little bundle of sewing tools wrapped in a piece of dirty cloth.

Meanwhile, I have been pushing my pillow very slowly under my blanket, little by little, so it will not be in view. But my hands become entangled in my scarf and I slip down.

Big Boot's flashlight travels to my mattress. I lie very still and try to disappear again. In my mind, I grow imaginary wings and fly away like my Jewish geese.

Big Boot shouts at me: "Hände hoch!" and I emerge

from the blanket and put my hands over my head. Big Boot steps on Sorele's and Tsipoyre's mattresses as he comes close to me. His fingers fumble with the buttons of my coat and he roughly touches my chest. I am thankful I have only nipples.

I have thrust my blanket aside, and it has revealed my pillow. The Hans Christian Andersen book has fallen out, and it lies on the mattress, mocking me.

Big Boot reaches for the book curiously. Perhaps he remembers one of these stories from his childhood? He once was a child, I force myself to think. He once smiled innocently and ran and played and did not know what a gun was.

I hold my breath, knowing that he will shoot me and possibly everyone in this room when my diary and my pen are discovered. Dr. Ringelblum, Batya, Gela, Estera, your names will be known. They will kill you, too! And Zayde and your prayers! They will know! And Gittel and Ruchel will be found out! The children's library at Leszno 67 will be known! The kitchen at Nowolipki 68 will be known! What will happen to the children? I force myself to form the most important question in my head — What will happen to the Secret Archive?

Suddenly, Sorele begins to scream. She is afraid that I will be hurt.

Her sobs draw attention away from me. Big Boot is angry. The only thing he sees on her mattress is her doll.

For a moment, he looks at it tenderly. Does he have a little daughter? But then the tender look is gone, and the angry look returns. His gloved hand swoops down, picks up the doll, and pokes her with his gun. Sorele's face is white, her mouth is open, and her eyes are wide.

Big Boot raises up Margarita on the butt of his rifle, slams her on the floor, and then stuffs her into one of his pockets, laughing all the while. Sorele cries and cries as though her heart would break. Tsipoyre goes over to her and hugs her. She rocks Sorele on her lap as she hums.

Big Boot shines his flashlight in Tsipoyre's face. Her hair sticks to her forehead from her sweat.

"No singing! No Jewish singing!" Big Boot proclaims.

Sorele is whimpering now, and Tsipoyre continues to rock her but is silent.

The other soldier who was so still comes to life now. Statue Man follows Big Boot out, stomping. We are once again plunged into darkness. Gittel and Ruchel hug each other tightly. Then they take a deep breath and let go of each other. They stand up and tie the scarves around their heads.

"We must leave in the darkness," Gittel says. "That soldier may return tonight or perhaps tomorrow ..."

Tsipoyre begins to sing:

Sorele, my little sister,
Zayde will sew another doll for you.
Her hair will be like Mama's—
Long and soft and silky.
Her buttons will be like Papa's eyes—
Round and dark and shiny.
Her face will wear Bubbie's smile—
Wide and full of wisdom.

Don't cry, my little sister—
Even if that soldier takes away another Margarita
    from you,
He'll never steal this song.
They'll never steal our songs.

Sorele stops her whimpering to whisper to Tsipoyre: "You got your singing voice back!"

Tsipoyre begins to cry now, more with relief than anything else.

Zayde reaches for his tallis from underneath his blanket. He kisses it and wraps it around himself. Then he creates his own prayer.

"Ribbono shel Olam, Master of the Universe. We are thankful to You that we are alive, not hurt. Thank You also for Tsipoyre's singing. Watch over us during these terrible times when we suffer like Job in Your Bible. Keep a special eye on Gittel and Ruchel. Amen."

Zayde gathers the six pillows he has made with the Warsaw Mermaid embroidered upon them. He stands up and hands three to Gittel and the other three to Ruchel. They reach for their knapsacks and put them inside. Zayde reaches for Gittel and Ruchel's hands and then hugs them both at the same time.

"Zay gezunt," he says with a trembling voice. "Stay well and keep well!"

And then, like cats, they are gone.

Tsipoyre is up for a long time, humming softly. Sorele falls asleep in her arms, and Tsipoyre carries her to her mattress. Then Tsipoyre goes back to her own mattress, where she continues to hum to herself until she is too tired. Zayde sleeps too, snoring with abandon.

I feel my eyes drooping, but I must capture what has happened on paper. I am worried about keeping my diary here. The room may be searched again. But where can I find a safe, secret place?

In the night, I unravel the rag that holds my pen and my Hans Christian Andersen book just to see if they are there. I can't get the stomping of the soldiers' boots out of my ears, even though the only sounds to be heard are Zayde's snoring, the rattling of the wind against the wooden boards of the window, and the cries of beggars. I hear a shot in the distance and wonder if another smuggler has been killed trying to climb over the wall. I pray for Gittel and Ruchel—Teresa and Rosalia.

To shut out the sounds and to calm the loud beating of my heart, I try to remember the merry-go-round horses. Then, in my mind, the piano music of Chopin ceases abruptly, and the horses stop their orderly prancing.

They neigh wildly and pull away from their harnesses until they are free. From the sides of their bodies, silver feathers begin to sprout like leaves.

One of them has the face of Janina, our goat. I stroke her beard and touch her wings. I sit on my pillow, with my treasure trove of words wrapped inside of the rags like a saddle, and Janina carries me away.

"Maaa-maaa," she sings to me until I fall asleep.

17 February 1941

IN THE KITCHEN at Nowolipki 68, I watch as Tsipoyre sings along with Estera and the children. Her face, her body, her entire soul is filled with expression.

Later on in the morning, I overhear Sorele singing to a scrap of cloth that she thinks of as her doll. She cradles it in her arms.

> *Zayde will sew another doll for me.*
> *Her hair will be like Mama's —*
> *Long and soft and silky.*
> *Her buttons will be like Papa's eyes —*
> *Round and dark and shiny.*
> *Her face will wear Bubbie's smile — wide and full*
> *of wisdom.*
> *And Tsipoyre will sing me a new song for my doll.*
> *And Rivke will tell me a new story.*

19 February 1941

I HAVE BEEN reading a library book I've discovered called "Birds of the World." I have learned that the albatross has long wings and can fly for a long time. It has webbed feet like a duck or a swan and lives in Australia. Flamingoes have pink feathers and live in South America. They like to stand on one leg, but they know how to fly. The ostrich lives in the Kalahari Desert of Africa and lays the heaviest eggs in the world. Even though it has many feathers, it cannot fly. But it can run very fast and kick very hard. Hummingbirds are the smallest birds in the world. Pigeons live in cities all over the world. Homing pigeons always know how to find their way home. During wartime, carrier pigeons acted as messengers by carrying important letters in their beaks. Are they serving as messengers during this war?

I worry about birds that might fly up against the barbed wire of the Ghetto and be killed.

I pray for Gittel and Ruchel on the Other Side. The soldier has not returned.

20 February 1941

GELA SEKSZTAJN WALKS into the kitchen while we are eating and waves at us. She says that she has come back to sketch our portraits. She asks us how we are.

Her eyes travel around the periphery of the room where Estera has taped up all of our pictures of the little match girl's wishes. Gela's smile grows very bright.

"Beautiful! So beautiful!" she murmurs.

And they *are* beautiful. The playroom is bathed in a canopy of colors.

Gela stays through the day with us. She captures our expressions as we finish eating, as we sit in a circle on the floor, as we sing, and as we read.

She holds a piece of charcoal carefully in her hand and draws with such concentration that I notice two lines in between her eyebrows.

I spend my time watching her draw. She draws Sorele sitting on Tsipoyre's lap. Tsipoyre's hair hangs over Sorele's chest as they rock together.

Gela draws Estera talking to us about animals in winter. "The bear sleeps," Estera says, and she pretends to be a bear, closing her eyes while she claps her hands together and places them under her cheek, like a pillow.

Gela places a piece of paper between each sketch so they will not become blurred or smeared.

She seems to have sketched everyone's portrait—all twenty children. I want to know why she has not sketched my portrait, but I want to ask another question even more.

"Where do you keep all of your drawings? How do you keep them safe?"

She is arranging her pile of pictures and pauses to look at me. Instead of answering me, she asks a question.

"Rivke—do you write down the stories that you tell to the children?"

I nod.

"How do you keep your words safe?"

I tell her about the Hans Christian Andersen book I hide inside of my rag pillow, but I worry about keeping it there. I say that soldiers burst into our room in the synagogue a few nights ago.

I want to tell her about my conversation with Dr. Ringelblum, but I promised him I would not tell anyone.

It is as if Gela can read my mind!

"Dr. Ringelblum told me about you, Rivke—about how he asked you to contribute to the Secret Archive," she whispers. I cannot say anything. I feel my eyes grow wide.

She looks at me intently and tells me that she wishes to show me something. She puts the pictures in her briefcase and stands up. She puts her coat on and wraps her scarf around her head and neck, the scarf that is the same beautiful blue color that makes me think of the sky. She looks at her watch. Then she tells Estera that she will bring me back shortly. I put on my coat and the scarf and gloves that Zayde has made for me. Tsipoyre is reading to Sorele and a few other children. I tell them I'll be back.

I follow Gela down the two flights of stairs wondering where she is going to take me. The drafts from the cold air slip through cracks in the boarded up window on the landing, and I brace myself for the gusts of wind that I know will ensnare us outside.

But Gela does not walk towards the front door! Instead, she turns left at the landing, and I follow her down the hall until we come to a door. She knocks on it lightly twice and then two more times. She opens the door and gestures for me to go down ahead of her. In the light from the hallway, I carefully walk down three of the steep, narrow steps. There is no railing. Gela closes the door behind her and says softly, into the darkness of the cellar, "Oyneg Shabes." I am grateful for the sudden light from someone's flashlight that shines its beams over the stairs.

At the bottom of the steps is a tall young man wearing an unbuttoned coat. His solemn face glows in the light from his flashlight. I have never seen him before.

"Nachum, this is Rivke," Gela says. I feel like I am in a secret world. I nod to Nachum and he nods back.

It is cold and damp. The ceiling is low. On the dirt floor, there are three mattresses separated by piles of bricks. The bricks look like low walls.

Gela turns towards another section of the cellar, and I follow her. Nachum walks quickly ahead of us — he seems to know just where we are going. Gela and I watch him push two bookcases slightly apart, and then he signals for us to enter through the opening. The bookcases touch the ceiling. There are folded rags on the shelves instead of books. We step into a little room.

Gela looks at her watch and says, "Give us fifteen minutes, Nachum."

Nachum nods, checks his own watch, and then pushes the bookcases back together again.

In one corner of the little room, there are ten metal boxes and two large milk cans. Against the back wall, there are bricks lined up to make a raised platform. A door has been placed over the bricks to make a kind of table. Rags cover sections of the door, and there are piles of papers arranged on top of them. A man standing near these papers kisses Gela on the cheek.

Gela introduces us. He is her husband, Izrael Lichtensztajn. Izrael smiles as though he recognizes me, but I don't know how this can be.

Gela takes off her gloves. She opens the lid of one of the metal boxes and takes out many pictures. This is her collection of paintings and sketches, she says. She will add the sketches from today to her pile.

When it is time, the Archive will be buried in the ground beneath it. When I contribute my diary, this room in the cellar is where it will go first.

I imagine my diary being placed in one of the milk cans and then buried in the ground. This thought makes my heart pound against my chest. I was cold before but now I feel like I am sweating. It is hard to breathe in the cellar and I feel my cheeks becoming hot. I take off my coat, scarf, and gloves. But I feel rooted to the spot like a stubborn seed clings to the soil, and even though my coat is heavy in my arms, I cannot move.

Buildings have layers the way that stories have layers. Like the skin of an onion. Who would have ever guessed that this was a collection point for the Underground Archive? Right underneath the kitchen where I spend time with the children!

Gela leads me over to a pile of bricks, and I put my coat on top of them and sit down. Gela says something to Izrael, and he brings a cloth to her. Gela wipes my face with the cloth and kisses my forehead. Then she reaches into the metal box of pictures. I can never forget what I have seen.

There is Zayde standing behind his cart on Gesia Street! He is still wearing his beard. The picture shows Mrs. Rotstejn wearing her apron and selling her potatoes, while Mr. Tuchman is selling his books.

In another picture, Zayde doesn't have a beard anymore. The people gathered around his cart have faraway looks on their faces; they are watching me as I am telling my story "The Jewish Geese." In the picture, my eyes are wide, my hands reach out, and my hair blows all around.

"You see," Gela says, "that day, when I heard your story in the marketplace, I couldn't stop thinking about it. I made most of these drawings over the next few days."

Then she shows me drawings of geese flying in a bright blue sky and landing in a field, where green grasses sway with the wind. There is the boy holding the shofar. There is the grandfather with his tallis around his head and shoulders. There are the geese with the Jews on their backs flying in the sky. I can see the rifle butts of the German soldiers as well as their helmets.

"Some of these drawings will go in our book, Rivke. The book we will make together. Batya told me about it. It is a wonderful idea! Your words and my pictures. I have been saving these two pieces of cardboard for the cover."

Then Gela looks at her watch. She puts her pictures and the cardboard back inside of the metal box and covers the lid.

"Come — I will bring you back to Estera now. Write up your story, and then give it to Batya, and she will give it to me. I will put the book together. Batya already mentioned that she gave you some paper."

I feel the tears welling up in my eyes. I have no words. It is like when Batya gave me the pen.

Gela's husband smiles at me again, and I realize he knows my face from his wife's drawings. I want to smile back but I am still so amazed I can hardly move my lips. He reaches out his hands to me and I let him help me stand up. He bends down and picks up my coat. He shakes my hand and says that it is an honor to meet the daughter of Chaim Rosenfeld. He knew Papa from various teacher meetings.

Even though I still feel hot, I follow Gela's example and put on my coat, scarf, and gloves so I can have my hands free to help keep my balance when I walk up the steps.

I watch as the bookcases are pulled apart by Nachum. How quickly the time has passed!

I follow Gela out. Nachum pushes the two bookcases back together again and closes up the secret room. I think of Izrael inside, carefully arranging the papers on top of the rags.

Then Gela reaches out to hug me, and I hang limply in her arms.

"I will tell Estera that you need to rest," she whispers in my ear.

She keeps her arm around me as we walk towards the steps. There is Nachum. He shines his flashlight on the staircase for us. He reminds me of Hans Christian Andersen's "The Steadfast Tin Soldier."

I follow Gela up the steep, narrow steps. She opens the door and gestures for me to stand in the hallway. Then she closes the door to the secret world.

We pass the front door on our way to the other staircase. Somehow I manage to climb up those two flights, but it takes a long time.

At the top of the stairs, Gela kisses my cheek.

"From one Ghetto artist to another," she whispers. "Now we share a special secret."

Gela takes my hand and leads me to Estera, who looks alarmed. They talk softly together until Gela leaves. Then Estera makes up a little bed for me with a blanket and some pillows. She gently takes off my coat, scarf, gloves, and shoes and helps me lie down.

Even though it is the afternoon, I feel so tired—like

it is the middle of the night. The children want to approach me, but Estera shushes them and has them play in another part of the room. Tsipoyre holds Sorele's hand, and they look at me anxiously.

Before I close my eyes, I glimpse the ivy plant growing on the windowsill. I imagine it grows into a great tree. Its roots reach deep down into the earth under the cellar of Nowolipki 68 and wrap around the milk cans and the metal boxes of the Secret Archive.

Later, when I awaken, my sisters sit near me and tuck in the blanket around my shoulders and feet. Sorele strokes my hair, while Tsipoyre gently touches the leaves on the ivy plant and sings to me in a voice like Mama's. It is as if she can read my mind.

> *Little seed in the ground,*
> *Grow, grow underneath the snow.*
> *Hold tight to your stem,*
> *Like a child to its mother's hand.*
> *Rise up, rise high,*
> *Green leaves touch the sky.*

24 February 1941

THE CHILDREN GATHER around me inside of Orphans Home, the orphanage at Chlodna 33 run by Janusz Korczak, Mr. Doctor.

I am telling them the story of "Thumbelina," about a woman who wishes for a child so much that she goes to a witch for help. The witch gives her a grain of barley to plant in a flowerpot. A beautiful flower with red and yellow petals grows out of the pot, and when the woman kisses them, they open up to reveal a tiny child—this is Thumbelina.

My favorite part is when Thumbelina thinks she must marry an ugly mole and live deep underground, never to see the flowers, the birds, or the sun. But there is hope for her! Earlier in the story, she has saved the life of a swallow who was frozen in a hole in the ground, and now he offers to help her.

I have memorized the words.

"Now that the cold winter is coming," the swallow told her, "I shall fly far, far away to the warm countries. Won't you come along with me? You can ride on my back. Just tie yourself on with your

> sash, and away we will fly, far from the ugly mole
> and his dark hole—far, far away, over the
> mountains to the warm countries where the sun
> shines so much fairer than here, to where it is
> always summer and there are always flowers.
> Please fly away with me, dear little Thumbelina,
> you who saved my life when I lay frozen in a dark
> hole in the earth."

Thumbelina ends up marrying the king of the flowers and receives a wedding gift of silver fly wings from one of the flowers.

The children clap when I am finished and pretend to fly like Thumbelina with her silver wings. Mr. Doctor asks me how I know the story so well. I tell him that I have a book of Hans Christian Andersen stories, and I have read it so many times that I know the stories by heart.

Mr. Doctor asks me to write down the story for him so that he can tell it to the children at night before they go to sleep. He offers me three sheets of lined paper and a pen. I accept the paper but tell him I already have a pen.

One child shyly tells me that her name is Anna and that she will write down the story in her diary. The children talk about keeping their diaries. Mr. Doctor is also keeping one. Paulina, one of the children, wants to see it. Everyone is curious. Mr. Doctor has us follow him to his small office. He picks up a notebook from under the charts on his desk and shows it to us. The children go to their beds and take their own diaries out from underneath their pillows or mattresses. Everything is surprisingly clean. Their diaries are bunches of paper bound together with tape or string.

They want to know if I am keeping a diary. I have been hiding my words for so long that I am afraid to talk about this out in the open.

"Yes," I tell them. Now Gela, Batya, Dr. Emanuel Ringelblum, Mr. Doctor, and these children know.

They want to see my diary, and I tell them that I'll return shortly and show it to them.

Mr. Doctor thanks me so much for coming—Batya told them about me. He wraps some children's books in a cloth and asks if I could please bring more the next time that I come. Stefa, his assistant, hugs me against her bosom and tells me that I am welcome anytime.

It is still early, about 10 a.m. I think about reaching for my diary wrapped in the rags of my pillow and showing it to the children. On my way to the synagogue at Nowolipki 27, I pass beggars on the street and children pulling along the fecalist's cart that is filled with our bodily waste. I pinch my fingers against my nose to block out the horrible smell. I see two Jewish policemen and a German soldier checking the identity papers of an old woman. She looks as though she has been detained a long time and has run out of explanations to satisfy them. I am hoping that now the old woman will be left in peace, when the pimple-faced soldier who stole Zayde's beard saunters by and pokes her with his gun. I hurry past—I cannot look at her desperate face.

When I arrive at Nowolipki 27, I smell smoke!

The door to the sanctuary is ajar. I see someone bent over the hearth throwing some rags on the weak fire. The person turns around to yank a loose plank of wood from the floor. I feel as frozen as a statue, like the time the Nazis came closer and closer to Zayde's cart before they ripped off his beard.

But this is a child! Our eyes lock together for a moment, and I see her dirty face become white with fear. Is she seven? Eight? She lets go of the wood and runs out of the sanctuary. Her fingers leave a trail of blood behind; her too-big shoes flop on her feet.

I turn to the smoldering fire and find rags there. Rags from our pillows! Among the rags, I find my diary. I hug it to my chest like it is my long lost relative. I remember how the Jews in my story hug the geese in the courtyard.

I finger the pages with my thumb. I have written in between the words of "The Steadfast Tin Soldier," "The Tinderbox," "The Snow Queen," "The Little Mermaid," "The Little Match Girl," "The Wild Swans," and "Thumbelina." I have six stories left: "The Darning Needle," "The Emperor's New Clothes," "The Red Shoes," "The Ugly Duckling," "The Princess on the Pea," and "The Nightingale."

The fire burns itself out. I pour water over it from the canteen that we keep in a corner of the sanctuary. Then I go to Zayde's bed and reach for his tallis that is underneath his torn blanket. I wrap the tallis around my diary and stick it under my coat.

My hair flies all around my face as I walk to see Zayde on Gesia Street. I have forgotten my scarf.

Zayde looks at me curiously when I show him my diary wrapped in his tallis, like a prayer. I tell him about the little girl who was so desperate for warmth that she came into our sanctuary to build a fire with rags. She would have even ripped up the floorboards if I hadn't come in just then.

Zayde pulls out a blanket from the bottom of the cart and wraps it around me while he sews a pocket inside of my coat for my diary. I worry about carrying my diary with me, but I don't know where else I can leave it. I will have to be very, very careful.

When Zayde is finished sewing, I put on my coat and gratefully slip my diary inside of the new pocket. Zayde looks at me more tenderly than before. He glances up at the sky and makes up a new prayer.

"Ribbono shel Olam, Master of the Universe. You gave my Rivkele a powerful gift of words. Grant her the courage to continue to write …"

He wraps a scarf from the cart around my head and neck and kisses my forehead. Then he folds his tallis and slips it under his armbands and pillows.

That afternoon, I return to Orphans Home to show my diary to the children. I feel like I give the children hope the way that Gela gave me hope when she showed me her pictures. Now Zayde also knows that I am keeping a diary.

Mr. Doctor points to the colorful pictures on the wall in the dining hall that doubles as a dormitory. They are all of Thumbelina and her silver fly wings.

I promise to write out the story for him.

Before Sorele goes to sleep, I tell her the story of Thumbelina. She cradles a new doll in her arms that Zayde has made for her. Her name is Thumbelina, just like the character in the story. At Sorele's request, out of the blue and white scraps left over from armbands, Zayde has sewn tiny wings on the doll's body. "We will pretend that they are silver," Zayde says to Sorele, who smiles at him.

Sorele falls asleep next to Tsipoyre, the new doll between them both. Tsipoyre sings this lullaby for Sorele:

Close your eyes, my little bluebird.
Dream about the clouds.
I'll weave a blanket of stars for you.
I'll stitch a pillow of prayers for you.
I'll plant you a tree where you can sing.

I fall asleep wearing my coat, touching the pages of my diary in the inside pocket.

12 March 1941

I FIND IT hard to take my eyes off of Zayde as he sleeps. I keep remembering what he told me tonight.

This is how the terrible day began:

Zayde is praying with a group of men in an apartment on Leszno Street that often serves as a place of worship. It is early in the morning, but the men cannot see the sun because they are praying in the cellar. A minyan of ten men are present. They are mostly old like Zayde. They sway back and forth, each of them wrapped in their tallis. It is the Fast of Esther.

Suddenly, three German soldiers burst down the stairs into the cellar. Although it is Zayde's turn to guard the entryway and let the others know if trouble awaits them, there is no time to give any signal.

The soldiers announce that the men must follow them.

There is a truck outside. Everyone is forced to climb into it. They manage to help each other do this. The men are driven out to the countryside. It is very windy. The snow upon the hills sparkles like jewels. The men wrap their tallises around their shoulders and pray that they will not be shot. When the truck stops abruptly, the men are herded into a barren field. They must haul rocks from one ditch to another, using their tallises to carry them. The rocks are very heavy. The men are not wearing gloves. It is very cold.

Zayde's fingers feel frozen. He sees some men who collapse on the ground and are whipped. A few of them do not move at all, and Zayde knows that they are dead.

Zayde comes home very late—after the 7 p.m. curfew. He falls onto his mattress with his dirty, torn tallis draped around his neck like a scarf. Sorele, Tsipoyre, and I hurry over to him. We take off his muddy boots and bring him the soup we have saved for him. His trousers are ripped at the knees because he had to kneel down to pick up the stones.

He massages his fingers until he can hold a needle. While he sews blue and white patches on the holes in his trousers, he speaks to God.

"Ribbono shel Olam, Master of the Universe. Thank You for keeping me alive to see my three beautiful granddaughters once again."

He kisses each of us, and we hug him so tightly he tells us that it hurts him.

After he kisses me, he puts his lips close to my ear.

"You must write about this, Rivke. Write about how their forced labor couldn't kill me. The love of my granddaughters makes me too strong for that. Today, in honor of Purim, I triumphed over another Haman!"

I close my diary and wrap it in the rags of my pillow. From under my mattress, wrapped in another rag, I take out the clean white paper that Batya has given me and get ready to write my story, "The Jewish Geese."

13 March 1941

ZAYDE, TSIPOYRE, SORELE, and I walk to the soup kitchen at Zamenhof Street 13 for the reading of the Book of Esther, the Megillah. We join in singing some Purim songs, and there is even some bread and a bit of marmalade to eat. Every time we hear the name Haman, we stamp our feet in defiance. Zayde's face beams.

14 March 1941

I AM DRAWN to the light of the early morning sunrise and step over all of the sleeping bodies to stand outside. The orange, red, and yellow glow is beautiful and speaks to me of spring. I see the Peddler of Wind shuffling by with his puppet and his sack. I think of the spring wind carrying the scent of flowers. The Nazis can't take away the sun or the wind from us. We are like Thumbelina emerging from the dark, underground cellar.

I write out the story "Thumbelina" for Mr. Doctor. When I give my story "The Jewish Geese" to Batya, she hugs me and promises to deliver it to Gela.

I worry about Gittel and Ruchel. I have not seen them for nearly a month.

17 March 1941

STORIES CAN COME into my mind so mysteriously. I wonder for a second if the Peddler of Wind really does carry fairytale wind in his sack.

Here is my memory:

In the afternoon, I sit on the cobblestones with the other children. We huddle together, wrapped in our coats, scarves, and rags. It is snowing. Spring seems very far away. Sorele holds my hand, and I look into her face and give her a smile. She smiles back from under her hat, and I feel warm for a moment. Tsipoyre sits on the other side of me. It isn't as cold when we are so close together.

Batya comes towards us, walking quickly. The snowflakes stick to her hair and her coat. She is holding a worn briefcase that I know is filled with children's books. She speaks to us breathlessly.

"I have just been speaking with Mr. Adam Czerniakow, Chairman of the Jewish Council. The children's library may now open legally! And Rivke, Gela has put your book together! It is in the library and ready to be borrowed. Rivke, gather everyone together and meet me at Leszno 67. You can tell stories inside. I will get the room ready for you."

Batya rushes away. For a moment, I am so stunned by her news that I can only blink. I have only been in the children's library very briefly to gather books to bring to the children, and I have only been there with Batya. How wonderful to be able to walk in and choose books from the shelves! And my own book will be among them!

Fayvel, the little violin player who has been sitting on the cobblestones with us, stands up and begins to play. We all stand up. The wind wraps itself about us, tugging at our clothes, and slipping through the holes in our pockets and our shoes. The wind carries the tune of Fayvel's violin, and it is a beautiful sound. When Fayvel adjusts his scarf, his violin bow slips from his fingers, and he runs after it. The wind has stolen it. But wait. Nu? Well? He is running back to us. He has gotten his bow back from the wind.

I stand up as straight as I can and stamp my feet, saying: "Go away, Wind!"

And then some of the children laugh. It sounds weak, as though the sounds in their throats have trouble emerging. But it is laughter all the same, and little hands holding cups or bowls shake the coins that lie there.

It is snowing faster now. Has the wind loosened the snow from the sky? It is a wonder to watch it fall. I try to catch some snowflakes on my tongue and soon, all of the children are opening their mouths, and some are jumping up and down. I stand still with my arms outstretched, gathering snow on my coat, on my scarf, on my hair.

The snow has brought a magic touch to our Ghetto. The cries and moans of beggars are hushed. The dirty streets look clean, whitewashed, covered with sparkling jewels. The rush of people slows down as everyone seems to pause and look up towards the sky. Even the wind subsides.

The gentle snow quietly gathers on our shoulders, on our heads, on the stars on our armbands, on the wall, on the barbed wire, and on the gates. I take a picture of the scene with my eyes.

The Peddler of Wind passes by slowly, his puppet in front of him, both of them holding their packs on their backs and selling their wind with the secrets. On the Peddler's head sits a pile of sparkling snow. A crown. He comes close to where we are gathered, closes his eyes, and then opens them quickly. He opens up his sack as well. "I carry wind wishes," he says softly. "But first, I bring magic bread for all."

After his puppet distributes the magic bread and the children stare at him, open-mouthed, the Peddler of Wind brings his hopping puppet over to each child, blue hat bobbing, as he whispers: "I carry wind wishes. What shall I pull out for you?"

Suddenly, Shmuel yanks off the Peddler of Wind's sack, and the man cries out in pain. Shmuel opens it and then swings it over his own shoulder and shouts: "There is no bread! There is no magic wind! No wishes! You and your puppet lie! All lies!" Then he turns away from us and runs down the narrow street. I follow him, trying to stay balanced on my shoes with the worn, uneven soles.

"Wait, Shmuel, wait! You must give him back his sack! It is all he has!"

He turns and throws me a look of disgust.

"You lie, too! Your story? It is a lie! No magic geese can come here to the Ghetto!"

And then he trips over a bit of ice in the street. He begins to cry. I go over to him. His shoulders are so thin. He allows me to put my arms around him.

"Listen," I say, and my voice sounds strong to my own ears. "This is a strange time. You can't just believe that what you see is true. If that were so, then all you'd see would be starving children and once strong men and women who look nothing like themselves. All you'd hear would be the moans of beggars or cries of children. If that's all you saw and all you heard, you'd feel even sadder and weaker than you are. But—if you let your heart listen to the stories, then their magic will bring a light to your eyes and energy to your step. And pretend bread is better than no bread at all.

"The stories will make you stronger. Like the bread you are able to smuggle past the German soldiers, Shmuel, from the Other Side. Let the Peddler of Wind carry his sack—he knows how to be the bearer of magic so that we can believe—if we only allow ourselves.

"And remember that pillow I gave you? Don't you sleep better now if you pretend there are feathers of wild geese inside of it instead of ugly rags?"

Shmuel nods and wipes his nose on his sleeve.

Just then, a German soldier comes towards us. I notice his big footsteps in the snow before I notice his uniform. Then something drops into one of the footsteps. It is a piece of candy. Shmuel picks it up with a question in his eyes.

"It's for you," the soldier replies, bending down and taking off his helmet. "I have a little boy at home, so I know that chocolate can stop the flow of tears." And the soldier smiles. It is a real smile, with his eyes smiling, too. Then, he stands up and crunches along on his boots until he comes to a young woman trying to keep her body covered against the cold. Her matted black hair sticks out in all directions. She looks like she was once pretty, a long time ago.

"Where's your armband?" the soldier's voice booms. Is this the same man who just smiled at Shmuel?

"I have it. It's right here," the woman says, as she points to the armband that she has wrapped around her neck like a scarf.

"On your arm! It belongs on your arm, Jew!" The soldier points at the armband around her neck with his gun.

The woman unties it and wraps it around her arm, trembling all the while.

"See that it remains there, Jew!" And then he spits in her face.

Shmuel waits until the soldier passes by. Then he walks over to the woman who is wiping the spit off of her face.

"Miss?" he says tentatively. "Here is something for you." He breaks off a piece of chocolate and hands it to the woman. She woman smiles gratefully. Shmuel catches my eye. I wink at him.

We return to the children and the Peddler of Wind sitting together. He is entertaining them with his puppet, and they are laughing.

Shmuel gives the sack to him, and he accepts it without a word, just a nod. Then the Peddler of Wind opens up this sack and pulls out scraps of burlap and other material, and he gives a scrap to each child. He shows them how to drape it over their fingers to make a puppet. His own puppet hops over to each child, blue hat bobbing, and the Peddler of Wind whispers, as before: "I carry wind wishes. What shall I pull out for you?"

As we walk towards the library, each child has a different request. In turn, they all hold their magical wishes—a butterfly, a flower, a bird, an apple, a leaf, a feather, a star. Tsipoyre holds her hands gently against her throat. She has wished for another song. When the puppet comes to me, I ask for some magic fairytale wind from far away. The puppet reaches into his sack, hands me some magic wind, and I close my eyes for a moment. When I open them again, I am seeing pictures in my head from another story.

When we arrive at Leszno 67, I bend down and scoop up a tiny bit of snow, and place it on the top of my index finger, which is wrapped in a scrap of cloth—the

head of my princess puppet. The snow is like a crown.
All of the children are silent — expectant. Shmuel seems
to hold his breath in wonderment. The Peddler of Wind's
puppet reaches into his little sack and asks the children
to throw me some more magic fairytale wind. They throw
some and blow some, and my princess puppet catches
their wind in between her tiny hands.

I open the door to Leszno 67. All of the children are
behind me as well as the Peddler of Wind.

Batya smiles at us and holds out her arms in welcome. Her glasses are perched on her nose, and she moves
them to the top of her head.

I notice that many of the books are no longer hidden in the back and sit proudly on the shelves. Batya
gathers piles of books from the floor and finds a place
for them on the shelves. The dolls and toys have been
placed on the windowsill to make more room for books.
So many books! I love to be surrounded by them.

We take off our coats and rags and place them on
the little hooks in the hallway. It is surprisingly warm in
the sun-filled room.

Batya silently points to the dark blue rug on the
floor. No one has yet said a word. When everyone is settled comfortably, I begin.

Once upon a time, in a faraway kingdom not too
distant from the sea, there was a princess who
longed to see the world. Her father, the king,
however, had barricaded his castle so that enemy

soldiers would never be able to enter. Besides the high wall all around the kingdom, the castle gates were always locked—all twenty-two of them. And besides that, there were two guards who stood at each gate, one on one side and one on the other.

The princess had her suite of rooms up in the attic of the castle. There she would sit, looking out of the highest window to the sea below. It was the only window in the castle that allowed the princess an unobstructed view of the world outside, for her father was so fearful of an enemy attack that he had the royal gate maker install iron bars across the other windows of the castle. Heavy curtains with heavy tassels hung over the windows and hardly allowed any light to shine in the castle at all.

The princess had asked her father to refrain from placing bars on this highest window by saying: "Papa, I will provide you with a very useful service. I will gaze out at the sea with the aid of the royal telescope, and if I should see any ships coming towards the castle without bearing your royal seal, I shall inform Your Majesty at once."

Now the king had a whole army of soldiers who were trained as spies for this particular work, but he thought that one more pair of eyes looking out for enemies couldn't hurt a bit. And so the highest window in the castle was the only one that provided a clear view of the world beyond. The princess loved to open this window and gaze all *about her with the aid of the royal telescope. It was a pleasure to breathe deeply of the fresh sea air, for all the other air in the castle was quite stale.*

The princess, whose name was Dalia, was not the only one who enjoyed this window. There was many a day that the royal cooks, royal coachmen, royal cobblers, royal seamstresses, and royal guards tiptoed up the rickety attic steps to steal a look and a breath. Everyone would immediately mop their neck and face with a handkerchief, breathe the cool sea air, and watch the gulls flying. The castle ovens didn't seem so hot, the horses didn't seem so taciturn, the leather for the shoes didn't seem so hard, the thread for the royal dresses didn't seem so coarse, and the royal marches around the castle didn't seem so stiff anymore. The royal workers returned to their jobs well refreshed. Even the pigeons of the kingdom came to peck for food on the roof of the castle near the open window. Every morning, Princess Dalia would throw out breadcrumbs to them. The pigeons came to trust her and would eat right out of her hand.

The king, whose name was Peter, heard about how the entire castle visited the attic window. He had a deep desire to see it for himself, but he was afraid. He was afraid that if he glimpsed the sea, memories of his wife would wash over him the way that the waves must have washed over her on that fateful day ten years ago, just after the birth of

Princess Dalia. The queen went for a ride in a small rowboat with two of her maidservants. Suddenly, a fierce storm came up, and they all drowned.

The king was afraid that he might slip on the stairs and fall down on the cold stone floor. He was afraid that he was not accustomed to such light and that it would be too bright for him, even if he were to shield his eyes. He was afraid that he might spot an enemy ship sailing towards the castle and then would really have to declare war. Most of all, the king was afraid that the view would be so beautiful that he would have to order that all the windows be opened in the castle to let in the sunlight. But then, with his guard down, he knew that his kingdom most certainly would be attacked. It had never happened, but he had to be prepared. And so the king stayed in his throne room and worried. Many times, he found himself closing his eyes and imagining the view from the highest window of the castle.

The princess imagined what the world looked like beyond her window. She read all of the books that sat on the shelves of the royal library and had many adventures in her mind. She spent many hours in her rocking chair and dreamed of rocking on the helm of a ship.

One morning, as the pigeons nibbled breadcrumbs on the roof, the princess could see that one of them had a red band wrapped around its leg.

*The princess unraveled the paper and saw that
there was a message.*

*"Dear Princess Dalia:
I am writing to you from the high seas. It is
beautiful and peaceful out here on the waves.
        Please write back to me.
                —One of Our Majesty's Sailors"*

*Princess Dalia wrote back right away and attached
the letter to the pigeon's leg with the red band.*

*"Dear One of Our Majesty's Sailors:
Which one are you?
        Can you tell me what colors you see on the
water when the sun rises? And when will you be
returning to port?
                —Princess Dalia"*

*The princess had the strong urge to paint. She asked
her servants to get her many colored paints and
wide canvases. She sent along more questions with
the pigeons for the sailor who had written to her.*

*"Dear One of Our Majesty's Sailors (I don't know
your name, but you are the one who wrote to me):
Can you tell me what colors you see on the water
when the sun sets?
                —Princess Dalia"*

Another letter read:

"Dear One of Our Majesty's Sailors (Once again, I don't know your name, but you are the one who wrote to me):

Can you tell me what colors you see in the sky during a storm?

—Princess Dalia"

While she waited for a reply, she dipped her paintbrush into colored paints and painted scenes of gulls flying and landing on faraway shores. She painted her mother, the queen, the way that she saw her in her mind, with her hair blowing and her face smiling when she went for her fateful boat ride, her royal crown glistening in the sunlight. Then the princess painted the terrible storm that churned waves all around the little boat while the two maidservants clung to their queen, to no avail. She painted her father, the king, sitting in his darkened throne room, his forehead creased with worry. She painted the castle guards, as she imagined them standing at attention outside the barricaded gates of the castle. She spent a lot of time imagining what the sailor who wrote to her looked like. She painted the wind rustling his hair and the feathers of the pigeons aboard. The princess painted the pigeons pecking at the breadcrumbs on the roof near her window, and she painted them nibbling out of her hand.

Finally, she received a message that was attached to a pigeon.

"Dear Princess Dalia:
The three pigeons arrived on the same day. Here are the answers to your questions:

The colors on the water when the sun rises are orange, red, pink, and a bit of yellow. When the sun sets, there are all of these colors, and the color purple. There are gulls that fly and seals that climb upon the rocks.

When there is a storm at sea, the sky is gray, black, and dark blue, and the winds are so strong that waves of the same color creep onto our ship.

My name is Joseph. We are returning to port any day now."

With the aid of the royal telescope, Princess Dalia saw His Majesty's ship sailing towards the castle. She wondered which sailor was Joseph. At the front of the ship was a statue of a dragon's head so frightful to look at that it would surely frighten away any evil spirits lurking in the blue-green waters.

King Peter was so curious to learn about the voyages of the royal sailors that he swallowed his fears of the light and the sea. Whenever these sailors returned to the shores of the kingdom, the king would eagerly greet them, even coming outside of the castle himself, with his long purple robes sweeping along behind him. He would blink—

the sun appeared to be so bright. Then he would quickly usher the sailors into the throne room while calling out to the guards to bar the castle gates once more.

"What do you see beyond our shores?" the king would ask the sailors.

Princess Dalia was allowed to listen to the stories of the sailors because she said: "Papa, it helps me with my paintings."

She painted the world that they spoke so enthusiastically about, especially the sailor named Joseph. His hair was red and curly like his beard. He had sparkling eyes.

The princess loved to listen to the songs the royal sailors sang about the sea. Every picture that she painted had a light glowing within it so that when they were framed and hung throughout the castle they looked like windows that revealed beautiful views. The palace workers didn't feel such a need to go up to the attic now that they could look upon these paintings. This time, it was the king who decided to see his daughter as she painted near her window.

One day, he climbed slowly, fearfully, up the rickety attic steps. He saw the princess painting him in a boat that was sailing far out on the open sea. "Ah," the king said to himself, "I cannot lock up the sea the way that I lock up the gates of the castle."

The light from the attic window surprised his

eyes, but he got used to it and came to enjoy gazing
outside at his wide kingdom. The king began to see
his foolishness. He ordered that the heavy black
window curtains and tassels be removed so that the
light could enter and shine on the paintings, and
they were even more beautiful.

The story of the dark castle that had been
barricaded for so long and was now filled with
light became known in many lands, because His
Majesty's own sailors told it to many people whom
they met in their travels. The princess gave some of
her paintings to the sailors to thank them for their
stories and songs of the sea, and her paintings
cheered them throughout their difficult and often
lonely voyages. The sailors brought pigeons aboard
and trained them to fly back to their ship.

The pigeons carried messages to the princess,
and when she held the pigeons in her hands, she
knew what kind of voyage it had been. Sometimes
their feathers were very cold, sometimes their
feathers were very warm, sometimes their feathers
were golden as though they had touched the sun,
and sometimes their feathers were gray as though
they had flown through smoke.

"Dear Princess:
Remind us to tell you about the dolphins that
swim in these waters. They try to jump upon the
ship with such a playful splash!
    My name is Samuel."

"Dear Princess:
The seaweed that covers the sand at high tide is like nothing we have ever seen before. It is green, blue, and dark purple. It sparkles. It tastes delicious.
My name is Benjamin."

The princess looked forward to receiving the messages that the pigeons delivered, and she always wrote back. Every morning, she checked the pigeons that came to peck at the breadcrumbs near her attic window. As soon as she noticed a red band wrapped around one of their legs, she unraveled the message right away.

But there came a time when the princess received no messages for many months. She wondered what could have happened to the sailors.

She painted them lost at sea. She painted them with frightened faces. All the while, the princess could only use dark colors.

One rainy day, when the princess was looking out of her window, she heard a tapping at the windowpane. She opened the window, and there was a pigeon with a red band wrapped around its leg. The pigeon shivered, and its heart beat wildly in its chest as the princess brought it inside the attic and dried its thin feathers. This is what the message said:

"Dear Princess Dalia:
I am writing to you near the shore of a beautiful

river. Not far away, there is a strange, dark, crowded city. There is a brick wall that separates one part of the city from another. The wall is topped with barbed wire. I hope that the pigeon I sent out could fly over it safely.

There are guards here at every gate, and people cannot move freely about. They have to wear an armband with a six-pointed star on their sleeves. There is not enough food or decent clothes to wear. People eat hard crusts of bread and wrap rags about them. We found out all of this with the aid of our binoculars.

We plan to dock here temporarily. We want to leave your paintings with the people who live in this strange, dark, crowded city. We believe that your paintings of the wildflowers, tall grasses, and trees that grow near the castle will give the people hope.

This has been a terrible voyage. We ran into a violent storm. Even now, as I write these words to you, I can hear the whistling of the wind.

—Joseph"

The princess wrote back immediately.

"Dear Joseph:
What a dreadful place! Be careful! I will send this message to you after the poor pigeon has had a chance to rest. I have been so worried about you and all the sailors.

*I am going to paint new pictures for the people
in that dark city. By the time that you return to
the castle, they should be finished.*
           —Princess Dalia"

Princess Dalia showed Joseph's message to King
Peter, and he ordered that big boxes be prepared
with clothing, shoes, food, and water.

    Joseph and the other sailors managed to
carefully wrap some of Princess Dalia's paintings
in burlap. Under a cover of darkness, some of them
left the ship carrying these hidden paintings with
them. They walked to the wall topped with barbed
wire. They managed to smuggle the paintings into
the cracks of the wall. On the Other Side, when
the people with the six-pointed stars looked at these
paintings, they held their breath and let it out
slowly, in their awe. The paintings, with their
reminders of freedom, nature, and bright, deep,
warm colors were very soothing to look upon and
gave the people hope.

    When Princess Dalia could see the sailors
returning to the castle with the aid of the royal
telescope, she alerted her father, King Peter. By this
time, Princess Dalia had quite a pile of paintings
she had made as gifts.

    The paintings were of toy trains, dolls that
looked like little girls and little boys, clowns with
bright red noses, and teddy bears with soft fur. She
painted more flowers and trees, this time with

birds singing in them. She painted fields of rye
and wheat growing plentifully, and she painted
many loaves of bread that had just been freshly
baked. She painted butter and milk, vegetables,
fruits, and cookies. The princess painted blankets
and shoes, hats and scarves, coats with perfect
pockets, underwear, and warm socks for children
and adults. She painted books that she had loved
to read in the royal library. She painted crayons,
paintbrushes, paper, and paints for the children.

When the sailors set foot upon land, the king
and princess welcomed them to the castle and
invited them to eat and drink in the royal dining
room. Then the sailor named Joseph gravely began
to tell the story of their journey, and the other
sailors joined in. King Peter and Princess Dalia
showed them the painted canvases and the many
boxes of food, clothing, and water.

After a restful night, the sailors started out,
carefully wrapping each painting in dark cloth, so
as not to call attention to them. They sailed in an
unmarked ship, painted black, without His
Majesty's seal, and with no sculpted dragon at the
helm. They brought some gold to bribe the guards
at the gates, if need be. They carried food, clothing,
and water in big boxes and brought them aboard.

The sailors who loved to sing sailed to this
distant shore barely uttering a word. The water
was calm and still throughout their voyage. Finally,
one night they arrived at the banks of the beautiful

river. Seven of the fourteen sailors picked up all of
the paintings that they could carry. With gold coins
in their pockets, they walked until they came to the
high wall with the barbed wire. Soldiers with
shiny boots and helmets followed them and asked
questions in a strange tongue, but the sailors did not
answer them. At the gates, the sailors bribed the
guards and then entered the barricaded place.
Everywhere they looked, they saw people begging.
The sailors turned to one another and began to
weep. "Why didn't we bring in the boxes with food,
clothing, and water?" they asked through their tears.
"Why did we bring the paintings first?" But there
was nothing that could be done at that moment, so
they handed out the packages of paintings.

The people wearing the six-pointed stars were
frightened. What was in those dark packages? The
sailors left quickly, making signs that they would
return. But on their way, the soldiers chased them
until they caught them. The soldiers entered their
ship and searched it, slashing open any packages
that they could see. The soldiers discovered the food
and the clothes, and they took them away, even
though the sailors fought back. But there were only
fourteen sailors and twenty-two soldiers, and the
soldiers won. Before the soldiers carried off the
goods in boxes, they climbed upon the mast and
slashed the sails of the ship with their knives,
laughing all the while. This made the sailors
sad and angry, but they kept thinking about the

suffering people they had seen on the other side of that wall. They thought of them all the while they had to sew their sails together, and this took a long time.

Meanwhile, the people behind the wall removed the dark cloth from the packages and saw the paintings. They spoke excitedly of some sailors who once brought in wonderful paintings that were filled with a light and now hung on the walls of the reading rooms, the kitchens, and the orphanages for the children to gaze upon.

"Yes! I have seen them!" said one child. "I have seen them, too!" said another child. "We have seen them, too!" shouted a group of children who recognized a painting that hung on the wall of their soup kitchen. The painting showed a castle that was not too far from the sea. A rabbi said the prayer for a beautiful thing since to gaze upon this sight was a blessing, and everyone said: "Amen."

Then the people reached out to touch the objects in the paintings, and the objects came to life! The dolls, the toys, the books, the musical instruments, the food, the clothing, the shoes— everything was real! The more the paintings were touched, more objects were revealed. Pigeons flew out of the paintings and out into the world.

The people with the stars on their armbands wondered about the mysterious sailors. Where did they come from? Who sent them? When would they come back?

"It is just like a fairytale!" said the children.
And so it was.

As for the princess, she never grew tired of
hearing the story about how the sailors brought her
paintings to the people, though she never knew that
the objects in her paintings came to life for them
and lasted until the end of the war. She longed to
visit the people herself and took off her royal crown
and dressed like a sailor, as did her father, the
king. But they both became so seasick that they had
to return to shore.

The sailors set sail again with more of Princess
Dalia's paintings for the people in that barricaded
place. They brought their pigeons with them. The
sailors never arrived, however. Some think that the
wind was so strong that it turned their ship in a
different direction, and they ended up in a distant
land. Others think that they drowned. Still others
think that some survived a storm at sea and made
their way here, to the Warsaw Ghetto, where they
live among us.

If ever you should happen to see a pigeon
pecking for breadcrumbs in the street or in one of
the courtyards, check to see if there is a red band
wrapped around one of its legs. Perhaps you will
find a message from the princess.

After the story, the children, the Peddler of Wind, and
Batya stare at me, barely breathing, it seems. We hear
clapping, and I notice Estera sitting there. She explains

that she was looking for some stories to read to us in the kitchen, but that the princess story is better than any in the whole library, except for "The Jewish Geese." She holds it up and then passes it around. "The Jewish Geese," by Rivke Rosenfeld, with illustrations by Gela Seksztajn. This is what it says on the cover. My heart beats so quickly just to look at it.

Then the Peddler of Wind opens the door and limps away. A blast of cold air slips into the library. Suddenly, all of the children begin to talk at once, and Batya, Estera, and I have to remind them to take turns.

Estera has more to say about "The Princess and the Paintings" story. She says that it makes her think about the story in the Bible about Noah. He sends out a raven from the ark, but the raven never comes back. After some time passes, Noah sends out a dove, which is really a kind of pigeon. The dove returns, but brings nothing in her beak. A little while later, Noah sends out another dove and when she returns with an olive leaf, Noah knows that land isn't far away.

The children want to pretend to fly like doves around Estera, who is supposed to be Noah, and they pretend to carry olive leaves in their beaks.

Riva, one of the children, says: "I think that the sailors helped the people escape to King Peter's kingdom. Little by little, they went in a ship until there were no more people in the Ghetto, and it made the Germans so angry!"

Then everyone wants to be a sailor. Very quietly, one by one, each sailor boy or girl tiptoes out from under the table that is their ship and escorts a person from the Ghetto to freedom. Suddenly, Moyshe picks up a pencil and makes circles in the air with it, around and around. "Alle Juden raus! All Jews out!" he shouts, pretending to be a German soldier, wielding his flashlight like a weapon. "Mach schnell! Quickly!"

We all freeze for a moment because it feels like real danger. Estera shushes Moyshe, reminding him to speak in a softer voice. We breathe a sigh of relief when Moyshe begins to laugh, and we go on with the game until all of the people in the Ghetto are saved.

Before leaving the library, Batya explains that everyone can take out two books—one in Polish and one in Yiddish. I feel too overwhelmed to search for any books at all. Instead, I help the children find what they wish to read. Many of the fairytales are borrowed. "Pinocchio," "Puss in Boots," "Sleeping Beauty," "Cinderella," "Jack and the Beanstalk," and others, too.

Since all of the children wish to take out "The Jewish Geese," Batya has decided to put it on display so that anyone can look at it inside of the library.

18 March 1941

IN THE KITCHEN, the story takes a new twist today when Pavlik, one of the children, says that one night, there is a terrible windstorm that swirls around the Ghetto. All anyone can hear is the harsh whistling of the wind. Then, a while later, people can hear someone singing songs above the whistling wind. It is a man who stands outside, his hands cupped around his mouth, singing words with a tune that goes up and down like waves. They are all songs of the sea that he knows from his life as a sailor and some new songs that he makes up that very night. As he sings, he calms the wind until the whistling becomes a hiss, and the hiss becomes a whisper. And then, all is silent.

So some of the children pretend to be the whistling windstorm enveloping the Ghetto. They dance around the room twirling their arms. Some of them pretend to shut their doors tightly to keep out the wind, and other children cover their ears because the whistling is so loud.

Then Tsipoyre stands up and begins to sing.

The wind is singing a song
And carrying it all around the Ghetto—
All around the world.
Perhaps my own words
Can fit inside this song
Like a warm pair of gloves
On a cold night.

Wind—can you hear me?
I am singing of seagulls
Circling the sky,
I am singing of mothers
Holding children
So they won't cry,
I am singing of beggars
Shuffling and passing by,
I am singing this song from my heart.

The wind is singing a song
And carrying it all around the Ghetto—
All around the world.
Perhaps my own words
Can fit inside this song
Like a pair of Shabes candles
Lighting up the dark night.

Little by little, the whistling wind stops, and the people uncover their ears to listen.

It is a beautiful song, Tsipoyre, I think to myself. Thank God you have found your voice again. We are blessed by your songs.

Dovid, one of the children, remembers the story of Jonah and asks Estera to read it. There is a copy of the Bible in the kitchen, so she reads it aloud. Everyone loves the part when there is a terrible storm at sea and the sailors are very frightened, but as soon as Jonah is thrown overboard, the sea becomes calm. Jonah ends up in the belly of a huge fish.

Sorele brings us back to my story by saying that Princess Dalia keeps rocking and rocking in her rocking chair; she thinks of the sea so much that she puts the chair on the waves, and it works like a ship! A magic wind blows, and she rocks all the way to the Ghetto on the sea!

Tomorrow, we will all pretend to act out the story from the beginning. I will be the narrator, and the children will take the parts of King Peter, Princess Dalia, the workers in the royal castle, the sailors, the pigeons, the guards, the soldiers, and the people of the Ghetto.

We will have three endings to the story—just the way some of the children have imagined it.

27 March 1941

THE STORY HAS kept us going for almost two weeks now. It seems to be all the children want to think about, and they want to present it to everyone in the Ghetto! Estera thinks it is a wonderful idea because she has never seen the children so absorbed in their play. Even adults are hearing about the story. Sometimes, when I am standing with Tsipoyre and Sorele next to Zayde's cart, people come up to me to buy a pillow, and they say that they have heard something about "this princess story." I smile. Zayde squeezes my hand as if to thank me for bringing customers to his cart.

The Peddler of Wind comes close to the cart too, with his little puppet. This time, the hand holding the puppet is still, and the Peddler speaks directly to me.

"I need some thread and some scraps of material. Do you think your grandfather may have any to spare? And do you think I may borrow a needle?"

His voice is smooth and clear—like a pebble rippling in a pond full of water.

"Yes," I say. "Yes, I think so. Let me ask him."

I speak to Zayde about the Peddler of Wind's request. He nods.

From underneath the pushcart, Zayde unwraps a piece of burlap and removes some small pieces of material. They are blue and white—leftovers from making the Jewish armbands. He pulls out the scissors that are attached to his belt, and he cuts off a bit of burlap and gathers the pieces of cloth into it. He ties a piece of red thread around the bundle. Then he reaches for his spool of black thread with one of the needles stuck into it, and he hands everything to the Peddler of Wind. The little puppet receives it all.

"Thank you so much. A sheynem dank." It is the smooth voice of the Peddler of Wind.

"It is my pleasure. Keep the cloth. Please return the needle and thread as soon as you are finished." My grandfather reaches out to shake the Peddler of Wind's hand, but they are both full—one with his little puppet, and one with Zayde's gifts, so they both nod and smile at each other.

The Peddler nods to me, and then he limps away. In my mind, I imagine that I feel a breath of fresh sea air against my face. Sea wind from my story. And just for a moment, the dirty scarf that wraps around the Peddler's head changes before my eyes into a sailor's cap.

I know the only surviving sailor who lives among us, I think to myself. He is a limping beggar who carries a puppet. I call him the Peddler of Wind.

2 April 1941

THE CHILDREN IN the kitchen are very busy now. Estera is very happy, she says, because the children come every day and more and more of them, too. Some children who spent their days begging on the streets are visiting the kitchen at least for a few hours in the morning. Many have families who depend on their begging to help them get money for bread. I picture a great swooping bird with sharp talons when I think of the word "bread."

Batya comes with fairytales from other lands. She reminds everyone that they are welcome to visit the library at Leszno 67. The children are drawing pictures when she comes, pretending to be Princess Dalia painting her magical paintings. When Batya goes around and asks them to tell her about their work, they want to give her a performance. When it is over, she claps and claps. The children bow. Sorele is smiling happily. She got to be Princess Dalia this time. And Tsipoyre's face is flushed with excitement. She got to sing her song again.

Before Batya leaves, she says that next month there will be a big celebration for "Month of the Child" — Batya says that Mr. Adam Czerniakow, Chairman of the Jewish Council, has declared this. If it is alright with

Estera, Batya asks me, would I consider narrating my princess story with the children acting it out for all to see?

"Yes!" I say immediately. "Yes!"

3 April 1941

EARLY THIS EVENING, Sorele, Tsipoyre, Zayde, and I attend an event in the hall at Tlomackie 5 in honor of the life of Yitskhok Leybush Peretz, who died in Warsaw twenty-six years ago tonight.

I feel Papa's presence throughout the entire program. Gela's husband, Izrael Lichtensztajn, says in front of everyone that Chaim Rosenfeld was a gifted teacher and an inspiring colleague. And a wonderful storyteller.

I notice people turning around to look at me and smile. I feel my face grow hot.

Mr. Lichtensztajn tells the story called "The Magician" that Papa always used to tell. Then he tells a story I have never heard before. It takes place during the time of King Solomon, and it is all about the wind.

> *One day, a woman who weaves nets for fishermen is so poor that she has nothing to eat—not even a piece of bread. Strong winds blow so hard that she cannot weave, and fishermen cannot venture out in their boats—it is too dangerous.*
>
> *The woman decides to bravely walk to a rich man's house a few kilometers away to beg for a loaf*

of bread. The rich merchant only allows her to go into his storeroom and gather up the crumbs of flour that lie on the floor. The woman gathers what she can and trudges home, battling the wind along the shore of her fishing village. On the way, she gathers twigs with which to make a fire.

She is able to bake three small loaves. She says the blessing over bread and is about to bite into one of the loaves, when suddenly a man rushes into her hut shouting that a terrible fire has destroyed everyone and everything in his village. He is the only one alive, and he is starving.

The woman feels she must give him the loaf. He thanks her and runs out of the hut. She is about to eat the second loaf when she is interrupted again—this time by another man who explains that his family has just been killed, and his property has been stolen. He is starving.

The woman gives the man the second loaf. He thanks her and runs out of the hut.

She is about to eat the third loaf, when suddenly a forceful wind pushes open the door of her little hut. The loaf that she is holding is torn from her hands and thrown into the sea.

After this, the waters are strangely quiet. Fishermen are able to go out in their fishing boats, and the woman is able to weave fishing nets again. Finally, there would be enough to eat.

But the woman is very angry. She can think only about how the wind stole her last loaf of bread.

She decides to walk to Jerusalem to tell King Solomon. Finally, she arrives at the palace. King Solomon, the wisest man in the world, listens to her story, and provides her with bread to eat and wine to drink.

In the meantime, three men have entered the throne room and are talking to the king. They are Arab traders of spices and jewels.

One night, they explain to the king, there is a terrible leak in their boat, and they have nothing that they can cover the hole with. "We screamed, we cried, we prayed," they say to the king. "We even prayed to the God of Israel and promised that if we were saved we would present this God with gold and spices." All at once, they tell King Solomon, there was a very strong wind. Then something blew into their boat and with great force plugged up the hole. They were saved! Now the traders wish to present their gifts of gold and spices to God.

When King Solomon asks the men what the hole was plugged with, the men show it to him. It is a small round loaf of bread. The king shows it to the woman, and she recognizes it as her loaf. King Solomon rules that the men should give their gold and spices to the woman.

The woman gratefully accepts the gold and spices. From then on, whenever she bakes bread, she always bakes extra loaves for those who may need them.

Afterwards, Mr. Lichtensztajn announces that, in keeping with the celebration of the evening and the story, everyone will be given a small piece of bread and jam. He asks us to consider giving our portion to someone in need on our way home.

As we walk in the street, I notice that many people share their bread with beggars.

When I see the Peddler of Wind shuffling by, I am overjoyed. I tell him the story we have just heard and then give him my gift of bread. Tsipoyre, Sorele, and Zayde offer him bread, too.

He says he cannot accept all four pieces. In the story, God knew to send one piece to each person who needed it.

Sorele and Tsipoyre eat their pieces of bread and chew in contented silence. Zayde breaks off a piece of his bread and shares it with me. I am just about to bite into it, when a strong wind comes along and lifts it from my fingers!

7 April 1941

WE HAVE BEEN very busy preparing for the play. Some of the children have been working on the scenery with Gela's help. She is sewing the costumes. Flayvel has been playing the violin in between the scenes for us. Tsipoyre has been a singing sailor leading everyone in song.

Batya has been watching our rehearsals with excitement. Lately, I haven't been able to go with her to visit with the children on the streets, in the synagogues, kitchens, or apartment buildings.

The play will be presented on May 5th! Mr. Doctor will be performing a puppet show with some of the children from his orphanage before our presentation.

There is also going to be a big exhibition — Thumbelina paintings, Little Match Girl paintings, and Gela's portraits of children.

I go to the library whenever I can to read any book that I can find about birds. I have read all of the bird books in Polish, and Batya is searching for more books about them in Yiddish. Sometimes I go with Tsipoyre and Sorele, but I love to go by myself most of all. I like to just sit by the window and look out at the sky, knowing that books, like friends, are all around me. The most wonderful thing is to see children I have met on the street sitting here inside of the library with books in their hands, especially "The Jewish Geese."

In the evenings, before it is dark, Tsipoyre, Sorele, and I walk with Zayde to the library run by Leib Schur at Leszno 56, where he lives. There is no room to sit and read there. Books are everywhere. I wonder how he and his friend can sit down or walk around, since the floor and the chairs are piled high with books.

Before we leave, Leib Schur shakes my sisters' hands very seriously, like they are adults. Then he looks at me very closely. I notice his bloodshot eyes with yellow bags under them. He coughs for a long time.

"Someday, Rivke, your words will be in many books in many libraries — not only the children's library of the Ghetto. And your stories will be translated into many different languages. Like the stories of Hans Christian Andersen. Allow me to shake the hand of the storyteller."

Zayde hugs him and pleads with him to take better care of himself.

"You care more about your books than you care about your health!"

But others who are hungry for books crowd into the apartment, and we must leave. Outside, people on the street walk quickly — we are all so afraid of being seen when darkness falls. The German soldiers are like birds of prey ready to swoop down and carry us away.

All the way home, I wonder what Leib Schur would say if he knew I keep my diary in between a book of Hans Christian Andersen's stories!

In the sanctuary, by candlelight, Zayde reads one of the books he has borrowed called *The Forty Days of Musa Dagh*, a novel about a terrible but true story, he says. It is about how the Armenians were slaughtered by the Turks during the First World War.

"It is a very popular book in the Ghetto," Zayde tells me. "Almost as popular as your story that is in the children's library." He smiles and winks at me.

Tsipoyre and Sorele look at "Sleeping Beauty" together. I look at my library book about birds and then turn to the book of folktales. Over and over again, I read the story from Japan called "The Boy Who Drew Cats."

I have read it so many times that I know it by heart, and I wish very much to share it. I begin by telling it to Tsipoyre and Sorele, but then Zayde puts down his book to listen, too.

Once, in a village of Japan, a boy lived with his parents and older brother and sister at a time when there was a terrible famine in the land. The crops did not grow, and the rain did not fall. The parents were worried about their youngest son. They decided to bring him to a monastery where he might live with the monks and do odd jobs for them. There, he would be assured of food.

The priest asked the boy three questions. The boy knew the answer to every single one and was allowed to stay. He did odd jobs like sweeping the floor and gathering firewood. He was a good worker, except for one thing. He would draw cats wherever he saw some blank space. He drew cats on the walls, on the floor, and even in the prayer books! The boy tried his best to stop drawing cats, but he was unable to do so. The priest told him that he would have to leave the monastery. It was clear that the boy's destiny was to draw. So the priest wished him well, gave him some food, and some advice: avoid large places, stay in small ones.

Then the boy packed up his drawing pen, his bedroll, and his few clothes. He walked towards another monastery that he saw in the distance. It was abandoned because there was a goblin that haunted it and frightened away all of the monks. The boy didn't know this, however. He started to sweep the sanctuary, hoping the monks would come back, notice all of his cleaning, and keep him as a novice. But night came, and they still did not come back. Surely, they would return in the morning, the boy thought, and he was so tired from all of that walking and cleaning that he decided to go to sleep. But then the boy noticed white rice paper screens all over the large prayer hall and couldn't resist the urge to draw his cats. He drew them in all different postures, and when he was finished, he looked back at them. They were so lifelike— the best cats he had ever created! He lay down on his bedroll in the middle of the large prayer hall when he suddenly remembered the advice of the old priest. He got up and saw that there was a small cupboard in a corner, and *he could just fit inside of it. He yawned, stretched, and went to sleep, closing the door to the cupboard behind him.*

In the night, he was awakened by a terrible screeching and shrieking. He couldn't imagine what the sounds meant. He was very frightened and trembled inside of the little cupboard but dared not open it up. In the morning, when it was very quiet, he cautiously emerged from his hiding place to find a huge rat-goblin lying in the middle of the floor of the prayer hall—dead! Then he looked around and saw that the cats on the screens that he had created the night before were dripping with blood. Blood was all over the floor, too. He realized that in the night, his cats had come to life and protected him from the goblin.

It happened that the goblin was the cause of the great famine. When the goblin was killed, the famine ceased, and the people of the land were very thankful.

The boy became a very famous artist known throughout Japan. All of his life, he especially loved to draw cats.

I fall asleep, holding my pen in one hand and the Hans Christian Andersen book in the other. I wake up in the darkness because I feel a gentle breeze blowing upon my face. When I open my eyes, I see Gittel blowing on me.

"Gittel!" I whisper, and hug her tightly. Her cross pricks my chest.

"I am not surprised to see you holding a pen. Are you writing down your stories?"

"Yes," I whisper.

"Do you write about me, too?"

"Yes," I whisper again. "And Ruchel."

"Ruchel is dead, Rivke. She was shot near one of the gates to the wall. Here is her cross and her baptismal certificate. Perhaps you will have need of them."

Gittel puts them over my head one at a time and tucks them into my shirt.

"Here are a few potatoes, Rivke. Here are some zloty from the pillows we sold. How Ruchel loved to tell your story! And here are some spools of thread—different colors for your zayde, and I have some bread, too.

"I always carry one of the Warsaw Mermaid pillows. So far, I believe it has protected me.

"Give my love to your zayde and your sisters. You are my shvester now, my sister—my mermaid sister. If we do not see each other for a long time, after the war we will meet in front of the Syrenka Warszawska, the Warsaw Mermaid statue, near the Vistula. Be strong! Be brave! I must leave you now to swim back to the Other Side."

I hug her again, and this time our crosses touch each other.

"God bless you!" we whisper, in between our tears.

And Gittel-Teresa is gone.

I keep touching the cross around my neck and the baptismal certificate. Finally, I take them off and put them into the pocket of my coat where I hide my diary.

Early in the morning, before I walk with my sisters to the children's kitchen, I notice that on the floor next to my mattress is a small drawing of a fierce cat. It is holding a shield in one of its front paws and a sword in the other. I cannot recall drawing it.

14 April 1941

WE HAVE A seder in the children's kitchen. Zayde has let us borrow some of his pillows to recline upon. He is happy with the beautiful colors of thread that Gittel brought for him. He hopes to make more pillows with scenes from "The Princess and the Paintings" story I have told him. He is sad to hear about Ruchel and prays for Gittel. I cannot talk about the cross or the baptismal certificate. Tsipoyre has made up a song about the things that Gittel has given us.

Potatoes, thread.
Zloty, bread.

Estera asks me to tell the Passover story. We eat matzah and potato soup. All of us enjoy singing the four questions, di fir kashes.

I also tell the Peretz story called "The Magician" that Papa always used to tell. The children wonder about the prophet Elijah. When will he come?

We spend a lot of time talking about the Pharaoh's daughter who saved Moses. Sorele says that the Pharaoh is like a king, and his daughter is like a princess.

Moyshe says he wishes there could be plagues against the Germans who invaded our country and who make us live in this Ghetto. There is the sound of slurping soup. None of us disagree.

22 April 1941

FOR THREE NIGHTS now, I have had the same dream about the Peddler of Wind. In my dream, I have to squint to see his face clearly. He is King Peter from my story. He is walking around his kingdom holding out his hands. His royal robes billow about him. He does not carry his puppet or his sack. I stop him and ask where he is going.

"I am looking for stories," he says to me, while his beard flies over his shoulder. "The princess has become ill and says that only stories can cure her."

"Stories to listen to or stories to tell?" I ask.

"I don't know!" he says. "That is like asking if I am buying or selling the wind!"

I wake up very early with the Hans Christian Andersen book on my chest and a pen beside me. I have been writing all over the margins of "The Princess on the Pea."

1 May 1941

THE CHILDREN HAVE asked that we charge two zloty so that the money can go to help the children at the orphanages and the kitchens. But they say that if someone doesn't have any money, they can still see the show.

We will be presenting "The Princess and the Paintings" in the hall of Dr. Korczak's orphanage at Chlodna 33. Mr. Doctor will be presenting his puppet show. It is based upon a fairytale that he created.

5 May 1941

ESTERA, BATYA, GELA, and I go to the orphanage early in the morning to put up the Princess Dalia paintings that the children have made to lend some atmosphere to our play. Gela insists that we post the title of each painting and the artist's name beneath it.

"It's like an art show!" she says.

The truth is that I have trouble concentrating on Mr. Doctor's puppet show. I am feeling so nervous about our presentation. I see so many people in the audience whom I know. Zayde sits right up front with Batya, Estera, Gela, and the children from our kitchen.

After the puppet show (which has a princess in it!), our kitchen group gets up and takes their places. Dovid and Moyshe unravel the long brown paper upon which is painted the golden castle. On the other side is a ship sailing on the sea.

The most wonderful part of the play is when Tsipoyre, a sailorwoman, sings her song. She sings it twice. It seems to me that everyone in the audience joins in. Many people put their arms around each other and sway to Tsipoyre's song.

Chairman Czerniakow stands up and thanks me

and all of the children from the kitchen for our presentation. "Perhaps we can present it again, sometime in the future, so that more people could see it?" he asks. "Maybe there will be another book for the children's library?" Everyone claps and claps. Then he says that the zloty that have been collected will go directly to help buy special delicacies for the children. Everyone claps some more. I keep thinking about the Peddler of Wind. Where is he? I have not seen him since the Peretz evening. I know he would have enjoyed our presentation very much.

After the play is over, I notice some adults coming up to Tsipoyre to shake her hand and thank her for her singing. Zayde kisses Tsipoyre and me on our foreheads and says the shehecheyanu prayer, thanking God for giving us life and for bringing us to this moment.

Estera, Gela, and Batya come over and hug us. Sorele comes too, in her royal cook's costume, and holds Zayde's hand.

Mr. Doctor asks if the princess paintings can remain posted in the orphanage for a month so that everyone can look upon them and "feel their magic." Estera says that she will ask permission of the artists, but she is quite sure that they would love to have their work exhibited.

I am rolling up the long brown paper showing the ship on the sea when Dr. Ringelblum walks up to me. He asks how my writing is going. I think about how I have already written in the margins and around the pictures of "The Steadfast Tin Soldier," "The Tinderbox," "The Snow Queen," "The Little Mermaid," "The Little Match Girl," "The Wild Swans," "Thumbelina," "The

Darning Needle," "The Emperor's New Clothes," "The Red Shoes," "The Ugly Duckling," and "The Princess on the Pea." I tell him that I have one story left. I tell him that I am worried about taking my diary with me everywhere, but I must, since I found my diary and the rags from my pillow in the hearth at the room in the synagogue where we live. I pat the new pocket that Zayde has made for me, inside of my coat.

He nods. Then he mentions that he has seen the beautiful book in the children's library—"The Jewish Geese." And Gela has spoken with him about me. He knows that I have seen the cellar, the milk cans, the metal boxes. He explains that when I am finished writing in my Hans Christian Andersen book, Gela will go down to the cellar with me so that I can deliver my diary. He thanks me again for agreeing to contribute to the Secret Archive.

He shakes my hand and then he hugs me.

"You have a wonderful imagination!" he exclaims. "I believe that someday the Archive will be discovered and your words—your stories—will live on and on, Rivke. Your contribution is invaluable."

I am in such a daze that I must sit down on one of the chairs after Dr. Ringelblum walks away. Thinking of my words buried under the earth makes my heart beat so fast with excitement that I can hardly breathe for a moment. I long to go with Gela to visit the cellar once again.

My name is Rivke Rosenfeld, I say to myself. Dear God, please let my words survive!

6 May 1941

IT IS A very long night. I hear Zayde moaning and tossing and turning, so I go over to him. He is sweating so much that his tallis sticks to his skin, and even his mattress is wet.

I put my hand on his forehead, then my lips. He is very hot. I bring him water from the canteen that we keep in the corner of the sanctuary. I raise it to his lips. He drinks it all and gasps for air.

What can I do? I say to myself. What can I do? I must get his fever to go down. But I am not a doctor. Even if I were, there isn't enough medicine or even beds for all the sick people in the Ghetto.

Hans Christian Andersen's story "The Nightingale" comes into my mind. I tell it to him softly, so I do not to awaken the others who are sleeping. All the while, I tell it to him with my hand upon his forehead, as if I am hoping to snatch up the fever and make it vanish. I remember how this was the only story I could tell when Bubbie, Papa, and Mama were so sick. Dear God, I pray, don't let Zayde die!

I notice that after I tell the story, Zayde is breathing

steadily and his forehead has cooled. He isn't sweating anymore. Has the fever left him?

I barely sleep myself, spending my time writing in this book. I imagine that our armbands with the Jewish stars rise up into the sky and shine their light over the Ghetto.

It is very early when Zayde calls me to him.

"Rivke," he says softly, slowly, speaking to me with his eyes closed. "I must have tea. I must have water and bread and vegetables and fruit that will help me get well. I am too weak to sew, and I fear the fever will return. There are no more armbands or pillows left on the push-cart. And besides, your Peddler of Wind has not returned my best needle, and without it, I cannot embroider pictures on my pillows. You must go outside into the market-place. Take your cup with you. Put it on the ground in front of you. You must tell your stories. Maybe some people who pass by will hear you and put a zloty or two into the cup. Take Tsipoyre with you. Let her peddle her songs. Sorele may come, but she must be told to listen quietly. Let us hope that people will pay for stories and songs with zloty."

When Tsipoyre and Sorele awaken, I tell them to dress as quickly as they can—Zayde is sick. They look at me with wide eyes and do as I ask, slipping on their shoes. Zayde is still sleeping. I ask Sorele if she will stay in the sanctuary with him in case he needs something. She takes her shoes off so that she can sit near Zayde and make less noise. I hold onto my cup with one hand and hold onto Tsipoyre with my other hand as we walk out of the synagogue together.

We go out into the early morning world of the street. The sun sheds its orange and yellow light as far as I can see. I think of Princess Dalia writing her letter to Joseph the Sailor and asking him what color the sunrise is out on the sea.

I tell Tsipoyre what Zayde has asked us to do. We watch as funeral carts roll down the street. Thin men with armbands pick up the small corpses that lie there for all to see.

I think of the Peddler of Wind and his little puppet that looks like him, both of them with sacks hanging over their shoulders. Aren't we all like him? I carry stories. Tsipoyre carries songs. Zayde carries prayers. Sorele carries her fierce love for us. The Peddler of Wind carries wind wishes. A passerby cannot see the special gifts we carry. They are invisible.

Buried in the pocket of my coat, next to Ruchel's cross and baptismal certificate, I carry my Hans Christian Andersen book and my pen. I have already begun to write in the margins of the last story. I told this story to Zayde last night—"The Nightingale."

I stand next to Tsipoyre at the corner of Gesia and Smozca Street. Beggar children come over to me from all parts of the street with hunger in their eyes. They are hungry for food, but they are also hungry for stories. They know

me from my visits with them on the streets, in the synagogues, the orphanages, and the soup kitchens. Some
are too tired to stand; their knees crumble and they lower themselves onto the ground. I am suddenly too tired
myself and sit down upon the bricks. I marvel at the sharp-
ness of them against my legs. Tsipoyre sits down, too.

I begin to tell the story of "The Nightingale" because
it is so fresh in my mind. Then I tell Peretz's story about
the bread and the wind. I feel that I sit for a long, long
time telling my own stories, Peretz's stories, and the stories of Hans Christian Andersen. Some adults have gathered near us, and they stand behind the children. No
one says a word. All eyes are on me. I hear a bird singing somewhere in the distance. Is the bird listening, too?

Suddenly, Tsipoyre stands up and starts to sing a
song of her own. It is my turn to listen carefully.

> *There is a tree*
> *Far away in a park*
> *Where a nightingale sings.*
> *I can hardly hear the song,*
> *But I know it is meant for me.*
> *It reminds me of a lullaby*
> *My mother once sang*
> *Long ago,*
> *When I was a little girl*
> *And did not know sorrow.*
> *But now, when I sing,*
> *My eyes are wet*
> *Like the morning dew.*

And my tears fall
On the wings of this bird
That I cannot see.

After her singing, the adults move close to my cup on the ground and put their coins inside of it. Then they walk slowly away. The children sit in front of us, lingering. They have no place to go. I feel exhausted and lean against Tsipoyre for support. Soon, I am sleeping.

When I wake up a little while later, Tsipoyre is counting the groszy and zloty that people have put into my cup. My cup is overflowing with coins, and I reach out my hand to touch them to see if they are real.

7 May 1941

IT RAINS DURING the night, and I am awake when Zayde calls for me. Tsipoyre quietly rolls off her mattress and goes to him. She gives him some water and he drinks, taking long breaths in between. She reminds him that we have apples, bread, and potatoes for him. We had to stand and wait in long lines for food, but the zloty gave us such comfort that we didn't mind waiting.

I touch Zayde's forehead. The fever has come back, but it isn't as strong as last night. I do not see any red spots on his body the way that I did on Mama, Papa, and Bubbie when they had typhus. I hope that the fever is fading from his body like the sickness that affected the emperor in "The Nightingale."

I think about what I have learned from my bird books. Nightingales are only six inches long and sing all through the day as well as the night. They live in Asia, Africa, and Europe. I have seen a picture of a nightingale. It is amazing to me that a bird with such a beautiful voice could have such dull brown feathers.

I ask Tsipoyre to sing us her song about this bird. Her words are like feathers in the air. She sings it softly, again and again, until she tires herself out.

I kiss Zayde's forehead. His fever is down, and he is breathing easily. It is a miracle. Or a coincidence. Or just a stroke of luck. I know that it will probably go up again.

Now Tsipoyre goes to lie down again, but I reach for my diary and continue writing until I am so tired that I can no longer grasp the pen.

8 May 1941

TSIPOYRE AND I start out to take our places on the street for another day of peddling stories and songs. For inspiration, I touch my diary in the inside pocket of my coat. I hold onto my cup with both of my hands. It is a magic cup to me now.

As we walk, I almost trip over a mound of rags. Something tells me to peer at them closely and take a good look. Someone has covered the face with posters printed for "The Month of the Child." The posters are torn. They say: "A CHILD IS THE HOLIEST OF ALL BEINGS" and "OUR CHILDREN, OUR CHILDREN MUST LIVE."

I recognize his hands first. Even before his long gray beard. His hollow eyes are sunken in his face and his mouth is open, but his breath does not rise and fall in his chest. There is the little puppet sticking up from his right hand; its hat has fallen off, and its tiny beard is streaked with dirt. It is the Peddler of Wind lying there. He must have starved to death in the night. Was he visiting with his grandmother like the little match girl in one of Hans Christian Andersen's fairytales?

And the sacks? What has become of the sacks?

Underneath the arm wearing the puppet, I see the sack that the Peddler of Wind always carried on his back. Gently, with Tsipoyre's help, I slip it out from under him. What is there inside of it?

Together we open it up. We pull out puppet after puppet. I recognize them all. There is the boy holding his shofar. There is his grandfather. And there are the little geese, with their feathers outstretched in flight. There are two peasants — a man and a woman — with their hands raised towards the sky. And there are two German soldiers pointing their guns.

There is Princess Dalia and her father, King Peter. There are three sailors and four guards. There is a pigeon with a band wrapped around its leg. There are two Ghetto beggars. There are two tiny paintings. And there is a puppet with a sack attached to its back with the embroidered words: "To the Peddler of Stories, From the Peddler of Win ..." Inside of the small sack is my zayde's needle and thread wrapped in a piece of burlap. I am reminded of the story "The Wild Swans," about how Elisa did not have enough time to complete the last sweater, and so her youngest brother ended up with half an arm and half a wing.

I bend over the Peddler of Wind and kiss his hollow cheek. Even though he is dead and cannot hear me, I speak to him anyway.

"Peddler of Wind — thank you for your gifts. How could you have made such wonderful puppets from mere scraps?"

We cover him up with the rags, and I lift the puppet from his hand and slip it into the sack. I know that other beggars will strip the rags from his body. I cannot bear to think of him lying there naked on the ground. I can only hope that someone with a funeral cart or wheelbarrow will come along soon to carry him away.

Tsipoyre helps me put each puppet back into the sack. I pick up the sack carefully and place it over my shoulder. I think about how the sack is wet when I touch it. Is it raining? But when I reach with my hand to move away the hair from my eyes, I realize that I am crying.

My stories and the stories of Hans Christian Andersen blur together on the pages as I write. I have only a few pages left. I promise myself to save space for the words I carry inside. I must talk with Gela tomorrow. I must save some space for my last words.

I think of the crane maiden before she is to weave her own feathers into a gleaming white cloth for the last time.

9 May 1941

ZAYDE IS WELL! He is sad that the Peddler of Wind is dead, but glad to have his best needle back. He sits in the sanctuary embroidering pillows with pictures of nightingales singing on the branches of trees.

I walk with Sorele and Tsipoyre to the kitchen in the morning, but my mind is very far away. All the while, I finger my diary in my inside coat pocket, and I carry the folded sack of puppets that belonged to the Peddler of Wind under my arm. My sisters gently point out the world to me.

Tsipoyre bends down, picks up a feather, and gives it to me. At first I think it has come from my own body. Then I realize that a bird must have dropped it. But is it a bird from one of my stories or a bird from the sky? I think of the birds I have known from the stories I have created and the stories I have read—a goose, a swan, a swallow, a crane, a pigeon, a nightingale …

Then, Sorele pulls at my hand and shouts: "Look up at the pretty blue color of the sky!"

And I remember how Gela helps all of us to see and feel color—outside, in the world of the Ghetto, and inside, in the world of our imagination. Of our heart.

In the kitchen, Gela is leaning against the door, laughing with Estera. I surprise Gela with the force of my hug—I am so happy to see her.

"I must talk to you *now*!" I whisper. "I have no more room!"

Once again, we walk down the two flights of stairs. Gela turns left at the landing, and I follow her down the hall until we come to the special door. It looks so ordinary, but I know it leads to a secret world. Gela knocks lightly on the door twice and then two times more. Then she opens it and gestures for me to go down ahead of her. In the light from the hallway, I carefully walk down three steep, narrow steps. Gela closes the door behind her and says softly, into the darkness of the cellar, "Oyneg Shabes." I think of Thumbelina, who hates the dark. I am grateful for the sudden light from Nachum's flashlight that shines its beams over the stairs.

Nachum quickly leads us to the two bookcases, and he pushes them apart so that we can enter through the opening. "Give us an hour, Nachum," Gela says, and looks at her watch. Nachum nods, checks his own watch, and then he closes up the opening between the bookcases. We are in the secret room.

The two milk cans and the ten metal boxes are in the same place as last time—in the corner. It is as though they are waiting for me to say goodbye to them.

Here I am, sitting on the floor of the cellar of Nowolipki 68, and Gela is beside me. I tell her that I want my words to be buried near her pictures. She smiles and nods.

I tell her the story of "The Boy Who Drew Cats", and she listens with her hand cupped under her chin. I ask her for a piece of paper, and I draw a cat holding a sword and shield like the Syrenka Warszawaska, the Warsaw Mermaid.

I say that I imagine Gittel Goldman as the Warsaw Mermaid mourning her sister. I give Gela the cross and baptismal certificate that Ruchel once held against her chest. It is hard to let them go, but I know I must. Gela reminds me that someone else will wear them and have a chance to live. Someone with blonde hair and blue eyes who is brave enough to travel over the wall. Gela lifts the lid of a metal box near the milk cans and places the cross and papers inside, where other crosses and certificates are already gathered. I wonder what other secrets lie on the floor here.

I tell Gela that after the war, Gittel hopes to meet me in front of the Warsaw Mermaid statue near the Vistula River. Then I take a deep breath and tell her the story I told to Gittel and Ruchel. When I am finished, Gela is quiet for a long time. Her eyes have a faraway look in them.

"If only we could all meet at the Warsaw Mermaid statue when the war is over …"

She rubs her stomach, and I notice how there is a little bump that I didn't notice before. Is she pregnant?

Suddenly, Gela pulls out a rolled up piece of paper, a pencil, and some cardboard from her knapsack.

"Rivke! I would like to draw your portrait! Would you hold still for me?"

I nod, cross my legs, and hold my diary against my chest. Gela straightens out the rolled up paper and attaches it with the tape that is already on the corners of the cardboard. As Gela draws, she leans on the cardboard, and I listen to Tsipoyre's songs in my mind.

When Gela shows me the picture, I blink. She has made my diary's pages open up as though with a magic wind, and little birds from my stories swirl all around my face. I am holding the book like a shield and the pen like a sword. My eyes are bright and bold.

"I will use watercolors later, Rivke. Thank you very much for sitting for me. It will be a lovely portrait—one of my best."

I am sorry when she takes my portrait away.

Then, Gela shows me some pictures she has painted of the children acting in "The Princess and the Paintings." For a long time, I look at the picture of Tsipoyre singing.

Now there is hardly any room between the margins. I hear the words of Mama, Papa, and Bubbie calling out to me in my mind—"*Live! Live!*"

And I wonder about my future. Sometimes I feel tired, weak, and sad. Other times, I feel angry. Like Shmuel, I get tired of pretending, of wishing, of imagining. But my words are as strong as they ever were. My words must survive!

I wonder—will the Secret Archive really be found someday? Will people read my diary? What will they think of my stories? What will they think of my sister's songs? And what about the special puppets made by the Peddler of Wind? Gela agrees that they belong in the Secret Archive, along with the stories that inspired them.

As I stick the feather that Tsipoyre has given me into this book, I allow my fingers to brush against the front of my dress. My nipples have started to turn into breasts.

I think of my diary placed inside one of those milk cans in this cellar and then planted deep in the earth. In my imagination, my words and the words of Hans Christian Andersen push up through a tiny crack in the dirt and turn themselves into wings ...

Acknowledgements

I wish to honor the memory of my late parents, Ruth Kaplan Pearl and David Pearl, who believed in me wholeheartedly. I am grateful to Bruce Black for caring about Rivke from the beginning and for his thoughtful, probing questions. Margaret Bush, Nomi Davidson, and Lucy Joan Sollogub offered me encouragement.

I would like to thank the staff at the Carnegie Library of Pittsburgh, particularly Joanne Dunmyre, librarian; Julie Horowitz, library assistant; Shayna Ross, library assistant, and Maria Taylor, librarian. I would also like to thank Marian C. Hampton, liaison librarian, Hillman Library, University of Pittsburgh; Dr. Heberer-Rice, director, Division of the Senior Historian, The Jack, Joseph, and Morton Mandel Center for Advanced Holocaust Studies, United States Holocaust Memorial Museum, Washington, D.C. Lawrence Kozlowski, chairman, Polish Nationality Room, University of Pittsburgh, and cultural commissioner, Polish Falcons of America; Justyna Majewska from The Emanuel Ringelblum Jewish Historical Institute, Warsaw, Poland; Tracy O'Brien, director, Library Services, Facing History and Ourselves, Brookline, Massachusetts; Mark

Seiderman, meteorologist, NOAA's National Centers for
Environmental Information, Center for Weather, Asheville,
North Carolina; and Liat Shiber, research assistant, Art
Department, Museums Division, Yad Vashem, Jerusalem,
Israel.

I would also like to thank my editor, Michael Mirolla,
and my cover designer, David Moratto. I am grateful to
all of the people from the Kiva community who uplifted
me with their support. I would like to thank my cous-
in, Sharon Nery, and my friends, Harry Bochner, Lucyna
de Barbaro, and Katherine Lancaster, for their astute
comments. I especially wish to thank my fiancé, Jack
Leiss, for his deep questions and thoughtful suggestions.

Author's Note

⌒

This is a work of fiction based upon historical events. Rivke and her diary are products of my imagination.

On September 1, 1939, the Nazis, who were in power in Germany under Chancellor Hitler, marched into Poland and took command of the country. This marked the beginning of World War II. The Nazis, with their symbol of the swastika, made new laws and the people had to obey even though the laws were cruel, unjust, and took away their fundamental freedoms.

On September 29, 1939, two days after Warsaw surrendered, the Nazis occupied the city. The Nazis declared that the city of Warsaw was to be split into a Polish quarter, a German quarter, and a Jewish quarter. On Yom Kippur, the Day of Atonement, October 12, 1940, a decree stated that the Jews of Warsaw, who were living in different sections of the city, had to move out of their homes and apartments and move into the Jewish quarter. Christians then moved into the homes where Jews once lived. The Jewish quarter became known as the Warsaw Ghetto.

By November 1940, the Ghetto was enclosed by a

brick wall eleven and a half feet high topped with barbed
wire. The wall was more than ten inches thick and elev-
en miles long. German and Polish police officers were
stationed at various gates along the wall. Jewish police
officers were feared and hated by the Jews of the Ghetto because it was their job to follow German orders. No
one could leave or enter the Ghetto without official papers. Jews were forced to leave their homes in various
Polish provinces, as well as different parts of the Ukraine,
to squeeze into the Warsaw Ghetto, until about 400,000
Jews lived there. On average, a single room was home to
seven people. Even synagogues became apartments.

Everyone aged twelve and above had to wear the
white armband with the blue Star of David. Even those
who converted to Christianity were still considered to
be Jews by the Nazis and were required to live in the
Ghetto and to wear the armband.

Jews of the Ghetto were subject to the arbitrary
whims of their Nazi captors. Jews couldn't be outside
after 7 p.m. (times of the official curfew varied) but
were so afraid to be detained that they were generally off
the streets earlier than this. Anyone could be made to
scrub the streets using only a toothbrush. Women could
be forced to use their underwear as a cleaning rag. Tallises could be used to clean toilets. Beards could be for-
cibly removed from men's faces like the way Zayde's
beard is taken from him. It was also dangerous to be inside. Buildings were routinely searched to frighten and
humiliate Ghetto inhabitants.

In the Warsaw Ghetto, Jews set up secret schools,

libraries, and places of worship. They had concerts, plays, and exhibitions. They found ways to listen to the radio and to write down their experiences in diaries. They smuggled food and news over the Ghetto wall.

The smugglers—many of whom were children—kept Jews from starving. In *Wordwings*, Gittel and Ruchel are teenage smugglers who "pass" on the Aryan side, mostly due to the color of their hair and eyes. Living on the Other Side was very dangerous because so many people were eager to betray Jews. Proper documents such as identity papers and work passes were necessary. Even then, sometimes the sad eyes of the Jews gave them away, according to Dr. Emanuel Ringelblum, a historian who became the founder and director of the Underground Archive of the Warsaw Ghetto. "Jewish eyes, the experts claim, can be recognized by their melancholy and pensiveness. The whole suffering of the Ghetto, the many years of torment, the loss of the family—all this was concentrated in them. It was told that a certain Aryan in a train spotted a Jew who had a first class Aryan appearance by his sad eyes" (*Polish-Jewish Relations During the Second World War*, pp. 103–104).

Ringelblum wanted to make sure that the history of the Warsaw Ghetto would be chronicled for future generations. Ringelblum's plan was to create an archive by enlisting people to write about their memories and experiences. These archival documents were to be collected and secretly buried in the earth. The code name for this archive was "Oyneg Shabes," which means "Sabbath joy" in Yiddish. Since paper was so scarce, some people kept diaries in the margins of books the way that Rivke writes in between the margins of a book of fairytales by Hans Christian Andersen.

The records that encompassed the Underground or Secret Archive embraced almost every aspect of Jewish life in the Warsaw Ghetto and were mainly in Yiddish, Polish, Hebrew, and German. According to *The Warsaw Ghetto Oyneg Shabes-Ringelblum Archive: Catalog and Guide*, materials were also collected in "English, French, Russian, Romanian, Ukrainian, and Italian" (p. 2). Ringelblum engaged many people to work with him to secretly write reports that dealt with religious, intellectual, cultural, social, and economic concerns. Ringelblum wanted the information to be presented as clearly as possible, and so he asked those from different perspectives for their insights.

The reports about the lives of children in the Ghetto were written by teachers in children's kitchens, orphanages, and clandestine schools. They were written by rabbis, doctors, nurses, and some children themselves. CENTOS, the Central Organization for the Protection of Children and Orphans, was a network of organizations created to help feed the hungry stomachs and spirits of children. The children's kitchen that I have Rivke and her sisters attend at Nowolipki 68 was one such place.

According to Barbara Engelking and Jacek Leociak, authors of *The Warsaw Ghetto: A Guide to the Perished City*, Nowolipki 68 was an important hub of clandestine activity. In addition to the children's kitchen, there was the Borochow School, headquarters for the Under-

ground Archive, and the site for publishing underground newspapers (p. 673).

In *Atlas of the Holocaust*, Martin Gilbert states that
the official daily allotment of calories in the Ghetto was
as follows: "Under the ration scales imposed by the Germans, all Germans in Warsaw were entitled to 2,310 calories a day, foreigners to 1,790 calories, Poles to 934
calories, and Jews to a mere 183 calories" (p. 53). I have
Rivke comment upon the juxtaposition of baked goods
displayed in shop windows while starving people peer at
them from the other side. Contrasts between rich and
poor were magnified in the closed world of the Ghetto.
Many children were left homeless and orphaned. Beggars roamed the streets. Some of them sang for a few coins
the way that Rivke and Tsipoyre peddle their songs and
stories.

Teenage girls, who traveled with false papers testi-
fying to their "Aryan" or Germanic background, collected information about life beyond the Ghetto wall.
Messengers from the Warsaw Ghetto were secretly sent
to various ghettos in other cities in Poland such as Lodz,
Krakow, and Lublin to learn about life there.

Over 250,000 Jews from the Warsaw Ghetto were
sent to the Treblinka concentration camp during the
Great Action or *Aktion* that began on July 22, 1942 and
lasted until September 12, 1942. On July 28, 1942, the
secret Jewish Fighting Organization was formed—
Zydowska Organizacja Bojowa—ZOB—with the determination to resist any further attempts by the Germans
to try to kill the Jews.

On January 18, 1943, when Jews were ordered to gather in their courtyards for another *Aktion*, they refused and went into hiding. The Germans met with Jewish armed resistance. The *Aktion* continued until January 22, and 5,000–6,000 Jews were captured. The *Aktion* was halted, but the Jews knew the Nazis would try to kill them again—they just weren't sure when.

During the next three months, Jews worked feverishly to construct secret hideouts called bunkers, underneath their buildings. They dug passageways between bunkers so that it became possible to slip from one bunker to another until the entire Ghetto was connected in this secret manner. Food, water, medicines, and weapons were hidden in these cramped spaces. Many people in the Ghetto had two addresses—one above the ground and one below.

On April 19, 1943, the eve of Passover, German soldiers strode into the Ghetto. They had orders to kill all of the Jews who were left. But the Jews had secretly warned each other to hide underground. The Ghetto streets were empty. From April 19 through May 16, 1943, the Jews hid out in their underground bunkers, defying the Germans, and some German soldiers were killed in confrontations with Jews. This conflict became known as the Warsaw Ghetto Uprising. The German soldiers had to resort to setting the buildings on fire so that the Jews were forced to emerge from their hiding places, only to be shot. Some Jews escaped from the Ghetto with help from the Polish Underground. In Israel in 1949, survivors of the Warsaw Ghetto Uprising founded a museum to

commemorate the Holocaust and the Revolt at Kibbutz
Beit Lohamei Haghetaot, Ghetto Fighters' House. The inhabitants of the Warsaw Ghetto would have been moved
to learn that the flag of the new state of Israel, established in 1948, carried the design of their armbands
— the blue outline of the Star of David against a white
background.

On September 18, 1946, ten metal boxes with archival documents were discovered under the rubble of the
building at Nowolipki 68. This discovery has become
known as Part One of the Oyneg Shabes-Ringelblum Archive. On December 1, 1950, two large aluminum milk
cans were found, also under the rubble of Nowolipki 68.
This second discovery has become known as Part Two
of the Oyneg Shabes-Ringelblum Archive. Material that
was buried under Swietojerska 34 was never located.

On October 16, 1985, in a sobering gesture heark-
ening to the burial of the Oyneg Shabes-Ringelblum Archive, two milk cans filled with ashes and soil from various concentration camps were buried during ground-
breaking ceremonies for the United States Holocaust
Memorial Museum.

One book that was especially important to me was
*To Live with Honor and Die with Honor! Selected Docu-
ments from the Warsaw Ghetto Underground Archives
"O.S." (Oneg Sabbath)* edited and annotated by Joseph
Kermish. *Life in the Warsaw Ghetto* by Gail B. Stewart
and the *Encyclopedia of the Holocaust* edited by Israel
Gutman were also very helpful.

The people mentioned in *Wordwings,* such as Batya

Temkin-Berman, Gela Seksztajn, Izrael Lichtensztajn, Leib Schur, Dr. Emanuel Ringelblum, Janusz Korczak, Stefa Wilczynska, and Chairman Adam Czerniakow, were important public figures at the time, and I have woven them into my story because Rivke knew them all.

Ringelblum wrote *Notes from the Warsaw Ghetto: The Journal of Emanuel Ringelblum* while he lived in the Warsaw Ghetto. He was killed in March 1944 with his wife, son, and a group of thirty other Jews when they were discovered hiding in a bunker in Aryan Warsaw. While in hiding on the Aryan side, he wrote *Polish-Jewish Relations During the Second World War*, where he described the work of Batya Temkin-Berman, children's librarian in the Warsaw Ghetto. As Rivke mentions in *Wordwings*, Batya kept her Warsaw Public Library branch open even after the city had been bombed. The book *Hunger for the Printed Word: Books and Libraries in the Jewish Ghettos in Nazi-Occupied Europe* by David Shavit, provided me with more details about her work. When the Ghetto was sealed, Leszno 67 was the address of a branch of the Warsaw Public Library. The books were supposed to be sent to the Aryan side of the city, but through Batya's determined efforts, the library was placed under the administration of CENTOS. It became a secret mobile library for the various organizations that served children in the Ghetto. Batya recruited a number of young girls, and she trained them to bring books to children on the streets, and in the orphanages, kitchens, apartment buildings, and other settings. I have Rivke become involved in this work.

In order to hide the actual function of the library, it was listed as the "Committee for Children's Games" for CENTOS (pp. 71–72). This is why dolls and toys were displayed on the shelves while the books were hidden. In the spring of 1941, the library became legal and about 700 child borrowers were registered. They were allowed to take out two books at each visit — one in Polish and one in Yiddish. Soon after the Great Action of July-September 1942, the children of the Ghetto were sent to the Treblinka death camp, and the children's library was abolished.

Batya escaped from the Ghetto in September 1942 and hid on the Aryan side. When the war was over, she returned to Poland, where she became the director of the Central Jewish Library. In 1950, she emigrated to Israel, where she died in 1953.

Leib Schur, who collected thousands of books and kept them in the apartment at Leszno 56 that he shared with his friend Barukh Mahklis, helped Batya gather children's books for her library. Schur's apartment also doubled as a lending library. He took his own life among his books on August 5, 1942, during the *Aktion*. (For more information about Leib Schur and Batya Temkin-Berman, see *Hunger for the Printed Word*, chapter three, pp. 55–78.)

Gela Seksztajn was an artist who worked with children in the Ghetto, teaching art and helping with costumes and scenery for their plays. She compiled over 300 drawings of children that were found in the Underground Archive. Her work is in the holdings of The Emanuel

Ringelblum Jewish Historical Institute in Warsaw, Poland as well as the United States Holocaust Memorial
Museum in Washington, D.C. One painting, titled
"Vase with Flowers and a Portrait," is on display at Yad
Vashem in Jerusalem, Israel. The quote that appears
near this painting is from Gela's Last Will and Testament and says: "As I stand on the border between life
and death, certain that I will not remain alive, I wish to
take leave from my friends and my works ... My works
I bequeath to the Jewish museum to be built after the
war. Farewell my friends. Farewell the Jewish people.
Never again allow such a catastrophe."

In *The Warsaw Ghetto Oyneg Shabes-Ringelblum Archive: Catalog and Guide*, it is noted that Gela's artwork
was placed in the metal boxes—Part One of the Archive
(pp. 288–311). In *Wordwings*, I have Gela's artwork and
Rivke's diary placed together in one of the milk cans.

Gela's husband, Izrael Lichtensztajn, worked as the
protector of the Underground Archive and along with
teenagers Dawid Graber and Nachum Grzywacz was re-
sponsible for burying the material. In his Testament, Izrael wrote: "I have thrown myself, with flaming enthusi-
asm, into the work of collecting material for the archive.
I have been charged with the role of guardian of the ac-
cess gate. I hid the material ... It is well hidden" (*To Live
with Honor and Die with Honor!*, p. 58). Dawid Graber,
aged nineteen, wrote: "I would love to live to see the
moment in which the great treasure will be dug up and
shriek to the world proclaiming the truth. So the world
may know all." And Nachum Grzywacz, aged eighteen,

stated so poignantly: "I don't know what's going to hap-
pen to me. **Remember, my name is Nachum Grzywacz**"
(*The Warsaw Ghetto Oyneg Shabes-Ringelblum Archive:
Catalog and Guide,* page following dedication page).

Izrael Lichtensztajn was also a teacher at the Borochow School that was located at Nowolipki 68. He told
stories by Yitskhok Leybush (known as Isaac Leib or I.L.
in English) Peretz, the famous Jewish writer from Warsaw, on a Saturday in May of 1941, as part of a larger
Peretz celebration that was sponsored by YIKOR, the
Yiddish Cultural Organization of the Ghetto (*To Live
with Honor and Die with Honor!,* pp. 445–446). I have
changed that date to April 3 in order to coincide with
the twenty-sixth anniversary of Peretz's death. It is believed that Gela Seksztajn, Izrael Lichtensztajn, and their
twenty-month-old daughter, Margolit, perished during
the Warsaw Ghetto Uprising.

The work of Dr. Janusz Korczak (this was the pen
name that he embraced — his given name was Henryk
Goldszmit) is discussed a number of times in the Oyneg
Shabes Archive, and he kept his own diary, *Ghetto
Diary.* Children of his orphanage shared excerpts of
their diaries with him. In an entry from late June or early July 1942, he quotes a child's words: "Szlama: 'A wid-
ow sits at home and weeps. Perhaps her older son will
bring something from his smuggling. She does not
know that a gendarme [police officer] has shot her son
dead ... But do you know that soon everything will be
all right again?'" (p. 158).

According to Betty Jean Lifton, author of *The King*

of Children: A Biography of Janusz Korczak, boundaries in the Ghetto were constantly changing. When the Ghetto was established, the Orphans Home was relocated from Krochmalna Street 92 to Chlodna Street 33, and in October 1941, it was relocated to Sienna Street 16 (p. 286).

Dr. Korczak was a medical doctor, orphanage director, and author of children's stories and of educational theory. The theater plays that he wrote in the Warsaw Ghetto have been lost, but his children's books, *King Matt the First*, the sequel, *Little King Matty and the Desert Island*, and the novel, *Kaytek the Wizard*, have been translated into English. During the Great Action, on August 6, 1942, Dr. Korczak, along with Stefa Wilczynska, Korczak's assistant at Orphans Home for thirty years, as well as eight other staff members, accompanied the 192 orphanage children to their death at the Treblinka concentration camp. Some of the children took turns carrying the flag of King Matt the First—a golden four-leaf clover against a green field. A blue Star of David against a white background had been sewn to the other side (p. 340).

Chairman Adam Czerniakow is also mentioned in the Secret Archive. He kept his own diary, *The Warsaw Diary of Adam Czerniakow: Prelude to Doom*. Czerniakow served as the appointed Chairman of the Jewish Council, which was like being the mayor of the Jewish community in the Warsaw Ghetto—except that he had to carry out the orders of the Germans. He had very little ability to exercise his own opinions or those of the community. On July 23, 1942, Czerniakow committed suicide because he felt that he could not carry out the German order that required him to deliver Jewish children to their death by having them gather in the *Umschlagplatz*, or transfer point, where they were to be taken on trains to the Treblinka concentration camp.

Czerniakow initiated the "Month of the Child" from late September to November of 1941 to try to gather more money from the population to help the children. The "Month" consisted of speeches and special performances designed to uplift everyone's spirits. Special posters were printed with messages such as "OUR CHILDREN, OUR CHILDREN MUST LIVE" and "A CHILD IS THE HOLIEST OF ALL BEINGS" (*The King of Children*, p. 284). In *Wordwings*, I have the "Month of the Child" occur in May of 1941.

The Syrenka Warszawska or Warsaw Mermaid has been an enduring symbol of Warsaw for centuries, appearing on official documents and the coat-of-arms for the city. Originally, she resembled a dragon-like sea creature with wings. Over time, she was transformed into a mermaid bearing a sword and shield. Her likeness is featured on souvenirs, signs, statues, and ornamentation on buildings.

The Syrenka Warszawska referred to in *Wordwings* is a famous statue that was erected near the Vistula River before the Second World War by the sculptress Ludwika Kraskowska-Nitschowa. Krystyna Krahelska, the poet who posed as a model for the face of this statue, died fighting in the Warsaw Uprising of 1944—a valiant effort by the Polish Underground to defeat the Nazis.

There are many legends about the Warsaw Mermaid. I have Rivke create her own story about her.

The stories "The Jewish Geese" and "The Princess and the Paintings" are also original. The stories of Hans Christian Andersen that are alluded to or described in *Wordwings* are "The Wild Swans," "Thumbelina," "The Little Mermaid," "The Little Match Girl," and "The Nightingale." I have retold other stories, including "The Magician" and "The Case Against the Wind" by I. L. Peretz, as well as the Japanese folktales "The Crane Wife" and "The Boy Who Drew Cats." Tsipoyre's song about the little boy who prays to God by playing a tune on his reed pipe was inspired by *Yussel's Prayer: A Yom Kippur Story* retold by Barbara Cohen.

At the United States Holocaust Memorial Museum in Washington, D.C., it is possible to see one of the milk cans that was part of the Oyneg Shabes-Ringelblum Archive. It is on loan from The Emanuel Ringelblum Jewish Historical Institute in Warsaw. When I saw the milk can at the United States Holocaust Memorial Museum, I couldn't get the image out of my mind. I kept wondering about the stories that could have been hidden within it. *Wordwings* is the result.

Selected Bibliography

⁓

Atlas of the Holocaust by Martin Gilbert. London: Michael Joseph Ltd., 1982.

The Boy Who Drew Cats and other tales of Lafcadio Hearn introduced by Pearl S. Buck, illustrated by Manabu C. Saito. New York: Macmillan, 1963.

A Calendar of Saints by Vincent Cronin. Westminster, MD: Newman Press, 1963.

The Case Against the Wind and Other Stories by I.L. Peretz adapted and translated by Esther Hautzig. New York: Macmillan, 1975.

Children and Play in the Holocaust: Games Among the Shadows by George Eisen. Amherst, Massachusetts: University of Massachusetts Press, 1988.

Children in the Holocaust and World War II: Their Secret Diaries compiled by Laurel Holliday. New York: Pocket Books, 1995.

A Commemorative Symposium in Honour of Dr. Emanuel Ringelblum and His "Oneg Shabbat" Underground Archives translated by Dr. Aleksandra Mahler. Jerusalem: Yad Vashem, 1983.

The Complete Andersen: All of the 168 Stories by Hans Christian Andersen translated by Jean Hersholt.

New York: The Heritage Press, 1942.

The Crane Wife retold by Sumiko Yagawa, translated from the Japanese by Katherine Paterson, illustrated by Suekichi Akaba. New York: William Morrow, 1981.

Encyclopedia of the Holocaust edited by Israel Gutman. New York: Macmillan, 1990.

Eyewitness Travel Guides: Warsaw by main contributors Malgorzata Omilanowska and Jerzy S. Majewski. New York, London: DK Publishing, Inc. 1997.

Ghetto Diary by Janusz Korczak, translated from the Polish by Jerzy Bachrach and Barbara Krzywicka. New York: Holocaust Library, 1978.

The Holocaust Museum in Washington by Jeshajahu Weinberg and Rina Elieli. New York: Rizzoli International Publishers, 1995.

Hunger for the Printed Word: Books and Libraries in the Jewish Ghettos in Nazi-Occupied Europe by David Shavit. Jefferson, North Carolina: McFarland and Company, 1997.

In the Warsaw Ghetto: Summer 1941, photographs by Willy Georg with passages from Warsaw Ghetto Diaries, compiled with an afterward by Rafael F. Scharf. New York: Aperture, 1993.

The Jews of Warsaw 1939–1943: Ghetto, Underground, Revolt by Yisrael Gutman, translated from the Hebrew by Ina Friedman. Bloomington: Indiana University Press, 1982.

Kiddush Hashem: Jewish Religious and Cultural Life in Poland During the Holocaust by Rabbi Shimon Huberband, edited by Jeffrey S. Gurock and Robert S.

Hirt, translated by David E. Fishman. New York: Yeshiva University Press, 1987.

The King of Children: A Biography of Janusz Korczak by Betty Jean Lifton. New York: Farrar Straus and Giroux, 1988.

Life in the Warsaw Ghetto by Gail B. Stewart. San Diego, CA: Lucent Books, 1995.

The Living Witness: Art in the Concentration Camps and Ghettos by Mary S. Constanza. New York: Free Press, 1982.

Notes from the Warsaw Ghetto: The Journal of Emanuel Ringelblum edited and translated by Jacob Sloan. New York: McGraw-Hill, 1958.

Polish-Jewish Relations During the Second World War by Emanuel Ringelblum, edited by Joseph Kermish and Shmuel Krakowski, translated by Dafna Allon, Danuta Dabrowska, and Dana Keren. New York: Howard Fertig. Jerusalem: Yad Vashem, 1976.

Polish Jews: A Pictorial Record by Roman Vishniac. New York: Schocken Books, 1988.

Resistance: The Warsaw Ghetto Uprising by Israel Gutman. Boston, New York: Houghton Mifflin Company, 1994.

Scroll of Agony: The Warsaw Diary of Chaim A. Kaplan edited and translated by Abraham I. Katch. New York: Macmillan, 1965.

Secret City: The Hidden Jews of Warsaw 1940–1945 by Gunnar S. Paulsson. New Haven: Yale University Press, 2002.

To Live with Honor and Die with Honor! Selected Documents

from the Warsaw Ghetto Underground Archives "O.S." *(Oneg Sabbath)* edited by Joseph Kermish. Jerusalem: Yad Vashem, 1986.

The War Against the Jews, 1933–1945 by Lucy S. Dawidowicz. New York: Holt, Rinehart, and Winston, 1975.

The Warsaw Diary of Adam Czerniakow: Prelude to Doom edited by Raul Hilberg, Stanislaw Staron, and Joseph Kermish, translated by S. Staron and the staff of Yad Vashem. New York: Stein and Day, 1979.

The Warsaw Ghetto: A Christian's Testimony by Wladyslaw Bartoszewski, translated by Stephen G. Cappellari. Boston: Beacon Press, 1987.

The Warsaw Ghetto: A Guide to the Perished City by Barbara Engelking and Jacek Leociak, translated by Emma Harris. New Haven: Yale University Press, 2009.

The Vanished City: Everyday Life in the Warsaw Ghetto by Michel Nazor, translated by David Jacobson. New York: Marsilo Publishers, 1993.

The Warsaw Ghetto: A Photographic Record 1941–1944 by Joe J. Heydecker, forward by Heinrich Boll. London: I.B. Tauris, 1990

The Warsaw Ghetto in Photographs: 206 Views Made in 1941 edited by Ulrich Keller. New York: Dover Publications, 1984.

The Warsaw Ghetto Oyneg Shabes-Ringelblum Archive: Catalog and Guide edited by Robert Moses Shapiro and Tadeusz Epsztein, translated by Robert Moses Shapiro, introduction by Samuel D. Kassow. Bloomington, Indiana: Indiana University Press, 2009.

Who Will Write Our History? Emanuel Ringelblum, the Warsaw Ghetto, and the Oyneg Shabes Archive by Samuel D. Kassow. Bloomington, Indiana: Indiana University Press, 2007.

Without Surrender: Art of the Holocaust by Nelly S. Toll. Philadelphia, PA: Running Press, 1978.

Yussel's Prayer: A Yom Kippur Story retold by Barbara Cohen, illustrated by Michael J. Deraney. New York: Lothrop, Lee & Shepard Books, 1981.

Notes

Quotes from the Hans Christian Andersen stories "The Wild Swans" and "Thumbelina" are from *The Complete Andersen: All of the 168 Stories by Hans Christian Andersen* translated by Jean Hersholt (The Heritage Press, 1942), pp. 115 and 36–37, respectively, from the fairytale section.

About the Author

Sydelle Pearl, a New Jersey native, currently lives in Pittsburgh, Pennsylvania. She has published books in genres including folktales, historical fiction, and biography. Sydelle is a former children's librarian who is a professional storyteller. She received a Storytelling World Honor Award for her book, *Elijah's Tears: Stories for the Jewish Holidays*, as well as a Freedom Through Literacy Honorable Mention Award from Judith's Reading Room for her author programs. Sydelle has presented workshops for educators at international, national, and regional conferences. Please visit her website, www.storypearls.com.